Trouble Afoot

With a resounding *thwack*, the door flew open and smacked against the wall. Mr. Levin, looking slightly dazed, poked his head in. *"There* you are! I've got to show you something."

He darted out the door. Harrison leaped up and ran after him. The others followed close behind, through the hallways and into one of the classrooms on their floor, the second. The windows overlooked the front of the school. "Take a look," Mr. Levin said.

A line stretched from the front door all the way down the sloping lawn to the street, then snaked at least half a block southward.

Harrison couldn't believe his eyes. "What the—?"

"Is that for *us*?" Brianna said.

"Oh, yes it is," Charles said. "Looks like our loyal fans haven't deserted us after all."

"I'm not sure it's that simple," said Mr. Levin, his tone wary. "But we'll talk later. Let's just get on with the show."

They started toward the cafeteria, with Mr. Levin at the end of the procession. Harrison held back a little, drawing even with the teacher. "You're not thrilled about this crowd," he said uneasily. "Do you think there's going to be trouble?"

Mr. Levin hesitated a moment before replying. "Don't you guys get it? There already is."

SPEAK

Published by the Penguin Group

Penguin Group (USA) Inc.

345 Hudson Street, New York, New York 10014, U.S.A.

Penguin Group (Canada), 90 Eglinton Avenue East, Suite 700, Toronto, Ontario, Canada M4P 2Y3
(a division of Pearson Penguin Canada Inc.)

Penguin Books Ltd, 80 Strand, London WC2R 0RL, England

Penguin Ireland, 25 St Stephen's Green, Dublin 2, Ireland
(a division of Penguin Books Ltd)

Penguin Group (Australia), 250 Camberwell Road, Camberwell, Victoria 3124, Australia
(a division of Pearson Australia Group Pty Ltd)

Penguin Books India Pvt Ltd, 11 Community Centre,
Panchsheel Park, New Delhi - 110 017, India

Penguin Group (NZ), 67 Apollo Drive, Rosedale, North Shore 0632, New Zealand
(a division of Pearson New Zealand Ltd.)

Penguin Books (South Africa) (Pty) Ltd, 24 Sturdee Avenue,
Rosebank, Johannesburg 2196, South Africa

Registered Offices: Penguin Books Ltd, 80 Strand, London WC2R 0RL, England

Published by Speak, an imprint of Penguin Group (USA) Inc., 2008

1 3 5 7 9 10 8 6 4 2

Copyright © Parachute Publishing, LLC, 2008
All rights reserved
CIP DATA IS AVAILABLE

Speak ISBN 978-0-14-241051-6

Printed in the United States of America

Drama Club Book 3:

Too Hot!

Peter Lerangis

speak

An Imprint of Penguin Group (USA) Inc.

Prologue

THERE'S A PHOTO OF ME OVER THE CASH REGISTER at Kostas Korner. I'm wearing a tight T-shirt, pack of cigarettes rolled up in the sleeve, hair slicked into a fifties-style ducktail, mouth wide open. I'm singing "Alone at a Drive-in Movie" from *Grease*.

To put the photo up, my dad, Gus Michaels (a.k.a. Kostas Michalakis), moved aside five autographed pictures of minor celebrities who've visited his diner. If you come for a meal, he'll point out my Danny Zuko photo. He'll also show you a copy of a review in our school newspaper, the *Ridgeport Rambler*, where Brett Masters wrote that I had "the best comic timing of any actor seen on the Ridgeport High School stage," and he'll go on to explain how the ancient Greeks invented the theater and how Telly Savalas was related to his mother's second cousin's wife. Then he will tell you who Telly Savalas *is* (a dead actor), before proudly reciting my GPA and observing that I'm better-looking than "Tom Cruisey." Then, if you haven't fallen asleep or run away, and I happen to be busing tables that day, he'll point me out and wave maniacally.

It's okay. I don't get humiliated easily. The thing is, my father hadn't wanted me to be in *Grease* in the first place—in fact, he forbade me, but that's a whole other story—so I'll take the positive vibes now. I'll need his support when I turn professional actor someday.

Which I plan to. Our high school, Ridgeport High on Long Island, New York, produces a lot of actors. You see them in movies, TV, and especially Broadway shows. People in Ridgeport can get a little ridiculous about the high school musicals. It's always been that way—the shows have big budgets and pep rallies, everyone's dying to get into the plays, etc. But it's gotten worse ever since the *New York Times* published an article about us, which basically said we were a breeding ground for Tony Award winners (btw, we have a shrine for them in the school lobby, just above the cast photos dating back to 1907).

The center of all of this is the Drama Club. I'm the president. My VP is Brianna Glaser. We've known each other since we were babies. Her family is rich; her mom works for some hedge fund and her dad's a business professor. Naturally, my dad the immigrant has always been angling for us to get together. Which we did, once, sort of. It was all very quick and strange and totally unexpected. That happens a lot when you do musicals.

Everyone is always so close and charged up. Sometimes you do things you would never dream of doing under normal circumstances.

I'm the guy who specializes in "character roles"—the bad guys, the older guys, the guys no one else can (or wants to) play. They keep telling me those roles always go to the best actors. They never put the word *looking* after *best*. The best-*looking* guys play the leading men—like Kyle Taggart, the RHS football star that Brianna recruited to audition. (Luckily, Kyle was a kick-ass performer. Unluckily, the girls fell all over him and nearly stopped talking to one another. Including Brianna. That's another story, though.) But I'm okay with doing character roles. I like the challenge. Mr. Levin, our faculty adviser, who used to be a Broadway actor, always says, "To be a success in acting, you have to check your ego at the door." Besides, I got a chance to be the star when I played Danny Zuko.

I have to admit, I liked the star treatment for a change. Pete Donner's little sister wanting my autograph. Lily Feeney touching my hand like I was a god. Her parents taking a picture of me so they could sell it "when I'm famous." The quiet guy who's been eating at the diner for ten years and suddenly wants to be my business manager.

But the whole thing got me thinking. About fame, but also about theater. Like why theater even exists. Like what's so good about it and why people go. I mean, when *Grease* was first written, it was edgy and daring. People thought it was vulgar and could never be done by high schools. *Rent* was like that, too, in the nineties. Some of

Shakespeare's plays were considered shocking, and have you ever seen *Lysistrata*, by Aristophanes? Mad weird.

Being shocked is cool. Seeing something you don't expect, something new that changes the way you look at the world—*that's* theater. You don't get that in, like, the 4,367th high school production of *Oklahoma!* But that doesn't mean it's not possible.

Anyway, that's what I was thinking in the weeks after *Grease*.

Maybe I was just bored with busing tables. Maybe it was the first day of spring. That can do things to your brain. Or maybe I realized that after playing Danny Zuko, I was probably not going to do the lead in the next musical, for fairness' sake.

Whatever it was, I got this strange idea in my head. And it grew into a funny kind of itch. And when that kind of thing happens to me, I can get really pushy.

So I pushed.

I wasn't trying to start a disaster. I wasn't thinking that I'd tear apart the whole town, not to mention the Drama Club.

I just thought it would be fun.

Part 1
Early Decision

March 31

1

"HARRISON, I DON'T BELIEVE YOU CAME OVER HERE to talk about this," Brianna said.

She sank into her sofa, arms folded. Harrison noticed her hair was blonder than usual, which meant that she'd had her annual March visit to Stuart Roberts Hair Salon — a surer sign of spring than the groundhog. Upstairs, beyond the curving mahogany staircase, Harrison could hear Siobhan the Nanny chasing around Brianna's little brother, Colter, for his bath. Brianna's mom and dad were at some fund-raising dinner, and the house had the feeling of a big museum of tasteful antiques.

"This is Drama Club business, Brianna, and you're my second in command," he said.

"*Your* second in command?"

"*The.*"

Brianna sighed. "Okay. You are hitting me where it hurts, Harrison. You know my middle name is Stupid Ideas. But this? Now? It's April already."

"It's March thirty-first."

"Silly me."

"This would be an unofficial play," Harrison said. "We don't have to get tied up with rules. Just a casual thing, because we love theater."

"Look, it's too close to the end of the year to do a play. Even for me. Official or unofficial." Brianna shook her head. "I mean, it hasn't even been two weeks since we closed *Grease*. Besides, you know what I just went through. Even if we *could* do a play—which we can't, because I know what Levin is going to say—but even if we could, I couldn't do it. I am burned out."

Harrison nodded. This wasn't a total surprise. Brianna was Type A+ to begin with, and as this was their junior year, she'd been piling on extracurrics and AP classes and a social life without limits. During *Grease*, she ramped it up, playing a lead while balancing a killer load of homework, SAT and AP prep, until she had finally snapped. Totally. It was scary. Everyone was worried about her—but she pulled through, and one of her resolutions was to cut back on the activities. Now Harrison was asking her to go back to the brink. He felt like a jerk for even bringing up his idea. "Sorry, Bri."

"I thought you were coming over to ask how I was doing."

"That, too," Harrison quickly said. "Are you okay?"

He sat down next to her on the sofa, upsetting the balance of the pillows so that Brianna slid closer to him. Her right thigh was touching his finger now. "Um, is this what I think it is?" she asked. "Because if so, Harrison, my little brother is still awake and the nanny is working, and I am so not in the mood."

"No!" Harrison sprang away. "How can you even *think* that?"

Brianna looked at him curiously. "Harrison, you confuse me."

"Me? Confuse *you*?"

"I was joking. Well, sort of. I mean, we should talk, Harrison. When a girl hooks up with a guy, especially someone she's known since she was a baby—"

"We didn't *hook up*—"

"Whatever you want to call it—anyway, sometimes she can't just pack it away like an unmatched sock."

Harrison sighed. They had been through this a hundred times. Something had happened. They had ended up on the sofa, during the rehearsal period for *Grease*. But things happened in the theater. When you were in the middle of a show, all the adrenaline going, emotions all charged up. "Brianna, we talked about this already."

"We said we'd cool it for a while. In Dude language, that might mean 'forget about it forever,' but in Girl, it translates into 'talk about it later.' And later does not mean by our thirtieth birthdays. Because after what happened during *Grease*, after my little experience with substances, after Charles rescued me from drowning at Jones Beach on a winter night and I had no idea how I got there, I've thought over *all* the days and nights that led up to my troubles. And you know what? That night with you and me—it was *not* one of them. I kind of liked it. And so did you. So why can't we talk about it?"

Harrison looked away, locking eyes with George, the strange, stuffed hoglike creature that her dad kept proudly on the mantel. This discussion was *not* what Harrison had come here for. "Yeah. I did like it, Brianna. A lot. It was just—I don't know, unexpected. Scary. We've known each other so long. You're like my sister."

"Scary isn't necessarily bad." Brianna moved closer. "And I'm not your sister. I'm not even distantly related. And we don't have to pretend it didn't happen. Because something *did* happen."

She was giving him a deep, significant look.

"Are you proposing to me?" he asked.

Brianna hit him with a sofa cushion. "I *hate* you!"

Harrison howled with laughter, rolling away from the sofa. "Look, I just came here to talk about a play!"

From upstairs came the sound of an enormous fart and a raucous peal of giggles. Colter ran downstairs, holding out a spent whoopee cushion. "Siobhan farted! Siobhan farted! Brianna, can you blow this back up?"

"Give it to Harrison," Brianna said, heading upstairs to do homework. "He has an inflated sense of self."

As Casey Chang searched for a spot on the lawn to sit, the pond echoed with the chuckly sounds of ducks. Around her, the eighth-period creative writing class settled in the grass, laughing, surrounded by the shy, sweet smell ıg. She could hardly believe her luck that Ms. ⏐uld take the class outside today. They were ⏐nit on playwriting, and today Ms. Ahmed was ⏐read some of the dramatic scenes they had slaved ⏐ weeks.

Casey stopped searching as she reached a patch of shade framed by two oak trees. Immediately a plaid-lined beige jacket appeared beneath her.

"It's wet," said Chip Duggan with a shrug. "The grass."

Casey smiled down at him. She always felt a little awkward about their height difference. Like it was somehow her fault that she was taller. But she was debuting a pair of spotless linen pants (a little tight, anticipating the weight that she was about to lose), and this was a very nice gesture on Chip's part. "You don't need to do that. But thanks."

"I have to wash it anyway," Chip said. "The jacket."

As Casey sat on the jacket's soft flannel lining, she smiled. It looked so . . . worn. But cozy-worn. She fought not to think of Brianna's evaluation of the Chip look—"so last year's Lands' End sale pages." Brianna didn't really *get* Chip. Not too many people did. He was intense, yeah—Casey had been trying to de-intensify him ever since they started seeing each other, during *Grease*. But he was that way because he cared so much. About the debate team, about the DC. And about Casey. Chip was sweet on the outside and soft-centered within. Like a Godiva chocolate truffle. Sometimes the wrapping was a little tight, that's all.

"If Ms. Ahmed reads my homework, I'm jumping in

the pond," Chip grumbled, removing a notebook and a graphing calculator from his L.L. Bean backpack and then sitting on the pack. It was custom-monogrammed ALD/RHSDT/SD for Augustus Lory Duggan/Ridgeport High School Debate Team/Superior Distinction—a fact he never admitted to anyone outside the team. Except Casey.

"Mine sucked, too," Casey commiserated.

"We'll suck together," Chip said. "Well. You know . . ."

He was blushing. And crinkling his nose. Which he always did when he was nervous. She liked that.

Ms. Ahmed spread her arms wide, closing her eyes and breathing in deeply. "This," she said with a smile, "is why we live." As she reached into her shoulder bag, her hair, a deeply lustrous black, flashed hints of cobalt blue. Which made Casey think of her own hair, which, no matter what she did with it, remained black like a coal mine. "Well, the good news," Ms. Ahmed announced, "is that none of your scenes were terrible."

Among the groans and nervous laughter, Casey could hear the padding of footsteps behind them.

"Nice of you to join us, Brett," said Ms. Ahmed.

"Sorry," said Brett Masters in a low, calm voice as he sat down with a sheepish smile. His hair was blond and shoulder length, and it blew gently in the breeze as if being arranged by invisible loving fingers. "*Rambler* meeting."

"Well, our esteemed school newspaper," Ms. Ahmed replied. "I can't object since your tardiness was in service of the written word . . ."

Brett smiled.

Dimples, too. What was it about dimples? Casey wondered.

Brett folded his long legs underneath him, flashing a smile at the half dozen or so girls who made room for him to sit. He was always surrounded as he walked through the hallways. He was like a conquering warrior, his shoulders slicing the air like blades, hair lofting behind him like a comet, a trail of brooding, black-clad girls in his wake.

It was a crime, really. Someone who looked like that simply should not be such a good writer. But he was. His poems were all over the walls of the class, and they made you cry. In case you missed any, he posted them to his blog, where they made you cry again. Plus he was the Drama Club Hero of the Moment, after his rave review of *Grease* in the *Ridgeport Rambler*—which included a mention of the "crisp stage managing." He flashed a glance of his deep brown eyes at Casey, smiling faintly.

"Well, it was a very good effort, class!" Ms. Ahmed announced. "Kudos! A couple of you moved me deeply." Ms. Ahmed was now pulling a set of stapled sheets out of her bag. "In fact, the first one I'm going to read was so polished . . . I have to admit, I Googled the heck out of it, just to be sure it hadn't been plagiarized. I'm happy to say it was not and I'm ashamed I ever doubted the writer."

Brett's shoulders slumped modestly, and he brushed away a lock of hair that fell in front of his face.

"Anyway, it's called *Early Decision*," Ms. Ahmed went on, "and if the author would like me not to do this, speak up now or forever hold your peace."

Brett wasn't protesting. He was looking out at the pond. Suffering in modest silence.

"Scene," Ms. Ahmed began. "Mid-February. Split stage. On one side, a suburban house. Mom and Dad are pacing the living room. On the other side, Winthrop— known as Win—is walking home from school. Win is lanky and slightly awkward, with a huge book bag and nice jeans. He's good-looking in a top-of-the-class way. A little jumpy. He stops before he reaches the house. He pulls a handwritten letter from his backpack. Reads it. His hands are shaking. He looks at the house. Thinks a moment. Then he rips the letter into tiny pieces. Sloppily. Some of the pieces fall to the ground. He throws the rest into a sewer. He stops before the front door to his house. For a split second he freezes. Closes his eyes. Looks like he is going to pass out. Then he pushes the door open.

"Now he is in the same scene as his parents. They turn toward him solemnly as he enters."

Ms. Ahmed looked up from the pages. "Do you see how the author really thought through how the scene would appear onstage? That's one of the things that separates a good play from a good story." She cleared her throat, and then went on reading.

WIN (*nervously*): 'Sup? Good news or bad?
Dad and Mom share an uncomfortable, unpromising look.
DAD (*shares*): Um . . .
WIN (*slumping*): Harvard nuked me, right? I'm sorry . . .
His parents look at each other again. Dad reaches into his rear pants pocket and hands him a letter. A big, thick one!

WIN (*oddly underwhelmed*): Hey . . .

His mom, unable to contain herself, throws her arms around him.

MOM: We're so proud of you!

DAD: We're taking you to the golf club. Ray Holberg
has a little something arranged. The guys at the law
firm are already planning your office space.

Mom pulls away from Win. He is totally without joy.

MOM: Look at him. He's overwhelmed. Win, why
don't you go upstairs and freshen up?

Win climbs the stairs. He turns to say something to
his parents. But they're poring over all the papers in
the envelope, talking about finances and law school.
He gives up. Goes to his room. Sits down at his desk.
Staring into space.

He shakes his mouse, looks at the screen. Then,
suddenly, he lowers his head to his desk. When he
rises, his eyes are vacant. Scared.

He rolls up his sleeve. And he takes out a pocket
knife.

Blackout. End of scene.

Ms. Ahmed put down the scene to total silence.

Casey could feel the tension all around her. She
recognized the sensation: an audience held in the
playwright's hand. She glanced at Brett. But he wasn't
taking credit. His face was scrunched up as if he, too,
were moved and upset.

"What do you think?" Ms. Ahmed said softly.

For a moment no one could muster a reaction.

"Does it make you want to know what happens next?" she pressed on.

Everyone nodded their heads and someone murmured, "Definitely."

"So what's wrong with Win?" asked Randy Schwartz.

"He's having a breakdown, of course," answered Jenny Fitz.

"I'm having a breakdown," said George Rubinsky, throwing up his hands. "My scene was nowhere near as good as that."

Ms. Ahmed nodded. "The scene asks more questions than it answers—that's one of the reasons it works. It leaves you wanting more. It has all the things we talked about—point of view, honesty, emotional engagement, real-sounding dialogue, pacing, suspense. It doesn't try to pack too much into one scene."

"Who wrote it?" Randy asked.

"Does the writer want to reveal him- or herself?" Ms. Ahmed asked.

Brett's head sank. But Casey knew. Everyone did.

Casey quickly took her eyes away from Brett. She had been staring. Smiling. Probably fawning, like every other girl.

It wasn't polite.

2

"HARRISON, WHAT HAVE YOU BEEN SMOKING?" asked Charles Scopetta, jumping down off the edge of the Ridgeport High stage as gingerly as he could, considering the extra pudge he'd gained since *Grease*. "I do not do tights or togas. And I definitely don't do *boring*. No offense, Harrison, I still adore you. But the DC hasn't done Shakespeare in five years, and for good reason."

"Shakespeare is not boring," Harrison insisted.

"I personally think it's a really hot idea," said Reese Van Cleve, who was moving to some unheard tune on her iPod.

Harrison smiled. "See? Reese appreciates real theater!"

"I appreciate boys in tights," Reese replied.

Harrison looked at Mr. Levin, the DC's faculty adviser. He had agreed to hold this special Drama Club meeting, even though Harrison hadn't told him why.

With a slight grin, Mr. Levin shrugged and said simply, "No."

"No?" Harrison repeated. Mr. Levin could be a prankster. He was a good enough actor to pull it off. His face—eager smile, big wide-set eyes, chiseled features, perfectly groomed salt-and-pepper beard—said *responsible and trustworthy*. But experienced DC members knew. A tug on the right side of his lip, a crease in the brow.

Unfortunately, at the moment he was untugged and uncreased.

"Do you mean *no* as in *no Shakespeare?*" Harrison asked. "Because that's cool. We can do something else—"

"I mean *no* as in *no play*," Mr. Levin said. "Not this year."

"Not that it's any of my business," said Brianna, slumped in an auditorium seat. "Because, as you know, I wouldn't be involved even if you *could* do it—but I just want to say as a general comment, there's this little problem of *planning ahead . . . ?*"

Harrison gave her his best we-don't-agree-but-you-didn't-have-to-torpedo-me glare. The trouble was that the rest of them—Charles the designer, Casey the stage manager, Reese the dance captain, Dashiell Hawkins the tech guy—would be influenced by whatever Brianna said. "It's April, guys," Harrison said. "We have three long months—"

"Two months, three weeks, and a day," piped up

Dashiell, who was deep into a game of Tetris on his laptop. "It's now April first, and school ends June twenty-fifth."

"I thought we were having this meeting to reminisce and gush about next year," Mr. Levin said. "Look, Harrison, we've just done two big musicals. Our budget has run out, the auditorium is booked solid for the rest of the year, and I am way behind on my English curriculum—"

"It doesn't have to be a major production," Harrison said. "This will be unofficial. Make our own rules. We can do something small. Creative and different. We don't need the auditorium. We'll do it wherever."

"We could do an improv," Dashiell said. "I could run a few comic-situation flowcharts. Shara, by the way, is a very gifted improv actor."

"Shara is gifted in a lot of ways," Reese said, giving Dashiell a sly smile that made him turn away. Shara was Dashiell's first girlfriend. Thanks to Shara, Dashiell was no longer attempting to seduce girls via Ritz crackers and Kraft cheese in a candlelit projection room.

"I have always wanted to do Oscar Wilde," Charles blurted out. *"The Importance of Being Earnest.* The wit. The style. The fabulous costumes. The tea."

"Charles, you are *so* weird," Reese said. *"I* see a story told purely in dance and music."

"These are great ideas, guys," said Mr. Levin. "Let's bring them up *next year.*"

Harrison slumped into a seat next to Brianna, and she patted his hand. "The boy tastes Danny Zuko," she whispered, "and now he wants the world . . ."

Harrison closed his eyes. He wanted to kill Brianna, but

he liked feeling her hand on his. Maybe they did need to talk. But the important thing was the play, and Harrison was watching that spiral down the toilet. He was a realist. Being the son of Kostas taught him that. You can serve the best moussaka in the world, but if your customers don't like eggplant, there's nothing you can do.

"Hey, Harrison, look," Mr. Levin said soothingly. "Maybe if we had decided on something by now, maybe if we had a definite plan, and thought it through—"

"Mr. Levin?" Casey interrupted. She leaned forward so suddenly, Harrison felt his seat lurch. "If we *did* have something, we could do it? I mean, hypothetically . . . if we had something ready to go—now—like, a totally original world premiere by an undiscovered teen writer? I mean, we could do that? That wouldn't be totally impossible, Mr. Levin?"

Mr. Levin cocked his head, a confused smile reshaping his beard. "Casey?"

"Do tell . . ." Charles's eyebrows were stratospheric.

"Just hypothetically," Casey repeated.

"Well, I suppose nothing's impossible, hypothetically," Mr. Levin said.

"Good. I mean, I think that's good. At least, hypothetically," Casey started. "There might not be a whole play."

She hooked her bag onto her shoulder and started into the aisle, muttering something about a big chem test.

And then she was gone, leaving the rest of the Drama Club wondering what she was talking about.

3

"IT'S AMAZING," CASEY SAID INTO HER CELL-PHONE headset, lying on her bed. "It's just so good, Brianna, you have to hear it. I swear, he is a genius."

"Or something," Brianna said.

Casey laughed. "Meaning what?"

"Gimme an *H*, gimme an *O*, gimme a *T*, *T*, *T*. Meaning, if Brett read the phone book, I would think it was genius."

"Brianna, I wasn't even thinking of that."

"No? Any guy who could get you to act like you did at that meeting . . ."

"Was I really bad?"

Brianna laughed. "Not really. In fact, you could afford to be a little more bad. So here's my question. If Brett has written this great play, why were you so vague? Why didn't you just tell the DC?"

"I don't *know* if he's written a whole play!"

"So ask him," Brianna said.

"I can't."

"*I* can."

"No!" Casey blurted. "He would know I was talking to you about him."

"Ohhhhh . . ." Brianna said knowingly. "This is about Chip, right? You don't want Chip to know you're lusting for Brett?"

"Brianna!" Casey could feel her face heating up. "I just don't know what to say to Brett. We're not really friends or anything. I don't even know if he knows who I am."

"You're blushing."

"How do you know?"

"Look. Brett mentioned you in his review, Casey. He *knows* you. And his screen name is Masterman0326. Send him a message. Pretend you need a homework assignment. Then work your way around to the point . . ."

"Right."

". . . That you're drooling over him in your dreams and you would like to, at the earliest possible convenience, jump his bones."

"Ha ha."

"But don't forget to close the message window."

"Why?"

"So when Chip sneaks into your room late at night, he won't suspect a thing."

"Good night, Brianna."

"It's seven-seventeen," Brianna said. "I will IM you at seven-forty-seven. That's plenty of time. You go, girl."
Click.

April 1, 7:46 P.M.
changchangchang: hi, brett. do we have hw 2nite for ahmed?
Masterman0326: yup. another scene. supposed to follow the first one chronologically.
changchangchang: ok.
Masterman0326: but it doesn't have to.
changchangchang: mm.
Masterman0326: l8r.
changchangchang: wait. i have a question. have u written a whole play? based on your scene? just curious.
Masterman0326: sort of.
changchangchang: sort of?
Masterman0326: yeah. u know me. i have like a drawer full of plays.
changchangchang: the dc wants to do an original play. maybe. do u want to submit? i can't guarantee, but they'll need to see it now.
Masterman0326: serious???
changchangchang: can u give me a rough draft, like tmw?
Masterman0326: i wd need to work on it. a lot.
changchangchang: by this wkend??
Masterman0326: ok ok. i'll try but i can't promise.
changchangchang: great!!!!!!!!!!!
Masterman0326: hey. btw . . .
Masterman0326: have you seen das shauspiel?

it's a german movie. at the regency. i may have spelled it wrong.

changchangchang: *no.*

Masterman0326: it's about putting on a show. i really want to see it. nobody wants to see it. it has subtitles.

changchangchang: *sounds great.*

Masterman0326: anyway, the dc shd check it out.

April 1, 7:47 P.M.

dramakween: *well?*

dramakween: *well?????*

dramakween: *im waiting . . .*

changchangchang: i dont believe it i dont believe it i dont believe it

changchangchang: he has a play. and he said yes!

dramakween: *i told you. now all u have to do is beg, bribe, or hypnotize levin.*

changchangchang: one more thing.

changchangchang: did u ever hear of a german movie about people putting on a show? i can't remember the title. like das schnitzel or something.

dramakween: *das schauspiel? did he ask u out to see that???*

changchangchang: NO! he just brought it up. said the dc shd see it.

dramakween: *that's code for asking u out.*

changchangchang: ha ha.

dramakween: *sweet dreams. i know what they'll be about . . .*

4

"WEASELS RIPPED MY QUIVERING FLESH ... ?"
Charles said to Brett with a barely disguised look of distaste
as he turned the corner on the second floor of RHS, along
with Casey and Harrison—and Kyle Taggart, hobbling
along on a crutch because of his ankle injury. "Your blog
is called *weasels ripped my quivering flesh?*"

"You didn't know that?" Kyle asked. "I thought everyone
read *weasels.*"

Brett laughed. "I got the name from my mom. It's based
on a title of an album she had in college."

"It's perfect," Kyle assured Charles. "Very evocative. Or
something."

Casey thought it was sweet that Kyle still hung out with
the DC, considering he was more interested in sports than
acting. Kyle, the jock who had the most amazing singing

voice, had become friends with them all when he played Jesus in *Godspell*. Even if theater hadn't really stuck, the friendships had.

"Wait." Harrison was staring at Brett. "Your mom suggested *that?*"

Brett shrugged. "She's pretty cool."

Casey smiled as they stopped in front of Ms. Ahmed's class. She had seen Brett's mom. She was stunning, which was no surprise.

Casey had looked up *Das Schauspiel* in an online dictionary the night before. It meant "The Drama." Brett hadn't brought it up today. Not that he'd had a chance. Not that she would say yes even if he did. But it was good to know.

"I talked to Mr. Levin," Harrison told Brett. "I told him we were going to have a scene reading from your play in my basement tonight."

"*Tonight?* I thought you said this weekend!" Brett glanced nervously at Casey.

Casey shrugged. It was the first she had heard of this.

"Mr. Levin just wants an *idea* of it," Harrison explained. "Just a few scenes. And he won't wait. If we're going to do this, we have to decide ASAP."

Brett shook his head. "Hey, look, I'm not ready for—"

The bell clanged overhead, and Harrison and Charles turned to go. "It'll be fine!" Harrison called over his shoulder. "And my dad's feeding us!"

"But—"

"Do it for the food, dude," Kyle said, propelling himself in the other direction on his crutches. "Then you can write it up on your blog."

Brett nodded numbly. He ran his fingers through his hair and ducked into the classroom.

Casey glanced back toward Harrison but he was booking.

This was all wrong. Why hadn't they told her they talked Mr. Levin into a reading tonight? She could have warned Brett. Maybe talked them into postponing this. Why was Harrison so bullheaded, so controlling?

As she headed into the classroom, Casey saw Brett smoldering in his seat, not even looking at her.

He hated her now, she knew it.

"Win . . .?" Ms. Ahmed's voice trailed off. The class was silent. Casey heard the ticking of the wall clock. Who knew it ticked?

"Win's mom comes closer,'" Ms. Ahmed continued. "Her son is rock-still at his desk, looking at his monitor. He does not answer. He is not asleep, nor does he seem awake. It is almost as if he has turned to stone."

MOM: Win? Are you all right?
She comes closer. Touches his shoulder. He doesn't react. Her eyes catch something. She leans over him. Squints at his computer screen. Reads aloud.
MOM (*reading what's on the computer screen, very softly, under her breath*): "I can't I can't I can't I can't I can't . . ."
She's totally baffled. Stepping back in surprise, she now sees that Win has a pocketknife in his hand. She leans down and takes it away. He doesn't resist. He's still a statue. Mom falls to her knees, still holding the knife. She wraps her arms around her son.

MOM (*screaming at the top of her lungs*): HA-
ROLLLLLLD!
End of scene.

Casey let her breath out. She hadn't even realized she
had been holding it.

"Reactions, anyone?" Ms. Ahmed asked.

"Win hasn't said anything, but you can feel what he's
going through," George Rubinsky said. "What happens
next?"

Brett nodded silently, barely noticeable. He wasn't
taking credit, wasn't answering questions.

"I think it works because it's . . . sort of, subtle," Jenny
Fitz said.

"Exactly," Ms. Ahmed agreed. "Its strength is in what it
doesn't do. Does a character come center stage and shout,
'Oh no, Win's having a breakdown!'? No, the writer *shows*
us the unraveling. By the character's actions. By what he
doesn't do. Are you all, like George, wanting to hear the
next scene?"

A murmur of assent went through the class.

"Me, too," Ms. Ahmed said, putting the scene down on
her desk and reaching for another. "Doesn't it make you
wish the writer had planned out the entire play?"

Sore subject. Casey glanced toward Brett again. And a
soft voice answered Ms. Ahmed's question.

"I did write the whole play."

Casey spun around.

It wasn't Brett's voice.

It was Chip's.

5

CHIP.

Chip had written the whole thing, not Brett.

Chip's play was the one she wanted to show the Drama Club.

Casey's brain was spinning. What had she been thinking? Why had she jumped the gun without knowing who the writer was? What was she going to tell Brett? She had no idea what Brett's play was about. Ms. Ahmed hadn't even read his scenes. What was she going to tell the Drama Club? *Why was everything happening so fast anyway?*

The bell rang. Chip, without looking at anyone, grabbed his pack and started out of the classroom.

"Listen, Chip, wait," Casey said, trying to keep up with him.

"I know, I know." Chip sighed. "It needs work."

"No—it's *amazing*," Casey said. "Everybody loved it. It's just that—"

"An artist," Chip replied, raising a cautionary finger, "should never be swayed by the approval of friends. Debaters learn this. You have to be objective. To listen and evaluate, as if the piece were written by someone else. And what I heard was melodramatic and sappy."

"Look, Chip, I did something really stupid," Casey blurted. "I promised your play to the Drama Club, well, a play to the Drama Club—it's a long story, and we're reading scenes tonight—"

Chip stopped in his tracks. "You *what?*"

The moment Casey opened her mouth to answer, Brett came loping around the corner, face deep in papers. "Hey, nice scene, Chipster," he said, looking up. "Casey, I have to talk to you. About the reading of the play, for the DC."

"*You know about it, too?*" Chip said.

Brett looked at him, puzzled. "Uh, yeah. It's my play."

"Um, actually . . ." Casey said. Oh God, now Brett was really going to hate her. How could she have been so dumb? "Brett, I made a huge mistake. I thought Chip's play was yours, that's why I IM'd you. I mean, I thought you were the one who wrote those scenes from class. That's the play the DC wants to do. Chip's play."

Brett stared at her. Chip stared at her.

Now they both hated her. Casey wanted to crawl into a corner. "I'm so sorry. I know you guys both probably want to kill me. I just—"

"No!" Brett cut her off. "This is perfect." He was

grinning. *Grinning!* "You don't understand—I mean, this is perfect. See, I kinda lied before. I don't really *have* a whole play. I have a few scenes and like, maybe a concept. But not a whole thing. I'm out. Use Chip's play! It's great. I'm more of a poet anyway. And a journalist."

"You mean that?" Casey said. "You're not angry?"

"Are you kidding?" Brett let out a laugh. "This is a huge relief! I was starting to freak about the idea of writing a whole play in like a month. I mean, I'm sure I could have done it, but you already have Chip's."

He was being polite, saving face. His feelings were hurt. They had to be. "Maybe you could write an article for us," Casey said, trying to be helpful. "Like, all about the DC . . ."

Brett cocked his head. "Maybe . . ."

"Not so fast," Chip grumbled. "I don't think my play is quite ready for a full treatment—"

"If you don't do this," Brett said, "you are crazy. If I could write like you, I'd do it in a minute."

"The DC will help you," Casey said. "Please? Come tonight, Chip. We're counting on you."

"Otherwise they'll just sit around and eat all that food without you," Brett said.

Casey checked the hallway clock. Thirty seconds till the start of chemistry. And Mr. Lingelbach was the kind of teacher who locked the door at the late bell.

Chip exhaled. His brow furrowed, as if he had just brokered a peace treaty. "Do I need to worry about things like staging?"

"No. We'll take care of it," Casey promised. "All we need

is a couple of printouts of the scenes for the reading."

Chip just looked up at her and smiled. "Can I give you the whole thing?"

"You are the best!" Casey threw her arms around him, gave him a kiss on the cheek, and flew down the hallway toward chem. "And so are you!" she called over her shoulder toward Brett.

6

"HEY, SEXY," CHIRPED REESE, READING THE PART OF Kayla, patient at the Gowanus Hospital for Adolescent Psychiatric Care from a copy of Chip's script.

The play was called *Early Decision*. Working title. Harrison was expecting a tame little play about college pressure, but not *this*. A killer drama about a kid's mental breakdown. Casey had been right. Chip was good. Really good.

The stage directions read *Win doesn't look up*, so he ignored Reese, using a toothpick to spear an olive and a stuffed grape leaf from a bowl. His dad always put these out whenever there were "guests" in the basement, even though no one below the age of twenty ever touched that kind of food—except Harrison. From the kitchen directly above them came the aroma of a Greek baked pasta dish called pastitsio, which Mr. Michaels had brought home from the diner in quantities large enough to feed the Spartan 300, and God, it smelled good.

Reese sat next to him. Waited a beat. Then she leaned closer and licked Harrison's right ear slowly.

"Yowza!" Kyle shouted from a beanbag chair in a corner, letting out a hoot of laughter.

Chip shot him a look. "It's in the script," he snapped.

"If you like it, Kyle," said Reese with a sly smile, "audition for the part of Win . . ."

"No auditions for me," Kyle said, thumping his cast-enclosed foot on the floor. "I have to sit out this one. My physical therapy for the ankle starts in a couple of days. After tonight, you guys don't see me after school at all for a few weeks."

"But tonight he'll sacrifice and happily eat the food," Reese added.

Kyle lunged forward and whacked her with his crutch.

"Dancer abuse," Reese grumbled.

"Can we keep reading?" said Mr. Levin, shifting uncomfortably on a small sofa, squeezed next to Charles and Chip. Dashiell and Shara were sitting against the wood-paneled wall, holding hands.

Harrison took a deep breath. His ear tingled. God, that had felt good. He crossed his legs and managed to focus on the script. The directions said *Win recoils.* Harrison recoiled. "'What the f—' Oops. Can I say that?"

Mr. Levin sighed and shook his head. "No."

"Don't you like girls?" Reese read, leaning in to Harrison. She was wearing a tight Danskin top, and the script said *She pulls a plastic bag of pills from her top,* so she pantomimed that. "And don't you like these? We could have a really good time . . ."

Win leaps up . . . Harrison leaped up from the chair, looking around nervously. "No! Get out of my room!"

Reese rolled her eyes and turned away. "Asshole!" She covered her mouth. "Oops! Bad girl."

"Harreeson!" bellowed Mr. Michaels's voice from upstairs. "You make sure everybody talk nice!"

"Don't worry, he knows it's a play," Harrison reassured him. "That's his idea of a joke."

Charles fanned himself with his copy of the script. "I need a shpritz. I'm exhausted from listening."

"Excellent," said Shara, her dark hair pulled back in a ponytail, which Dashiell was twirling idly in his hands.

"Indeed," said Dashiell.

"It's really good, Chip," Harrison said enthusiastically. But Chip looked pale. Next to him, Mr. Levin sat sphinxlike, without expression. "Um . . . let's do some more before we eat?"

"I think we should break for dinner," Mr. Levin said.

"But we haven't finished," Harrison said. "You need to hear the end."

"Oh, I've read the whole thing," Mr. Levin replied.

Already? Harrison swallowed. "And . . . ?"

"Well, the language is . . . harsh," Mr. Levin said, sitting forward slowly.

"But it's the way people speak," Chip protested. "As

Ms. Ahmed says, for a play to be true, the dialogue must be both intense and real."

Harrison looked at Casey, who was absently destroying her fingernails.

"Dear Chip . . ." Mr. Levin said, looking at the floor. "Dear, talented, defensive Chip . . ."

His voice trailed off. Chip bit his lip. He looked like he was about to cry.

"It would be an administrative nightmare to pull this together in such a short time," said Mr. Levin.

"Not really," Dashiell said. "We could do it on a bare-bones budget. Keep the staging and lighting simple, minimalist. And if we bill it as a play by a student, a first-time writer, it could be sort of experimental, unofficial. We would keep the level of expectation down."

"Exactly," Harrison said. "Almost like something from a workshop, rather than a big, formal production. A work in progress!"

"Which it is," Mr. Levin reminded them. "This play still has some rough spots." He lifted his head, his eyes meeting Chip's. "But to be honest, guy, I really can't see any way *not* to do this."

Chip opened his mouth, ready to protest, then stopped.

"Can't not?" Charles murmured. "Did he say 'can't not'? I always get confused when people use double negatives."

"It's lean, it's interesting, it's about something real," Mr. Levin said, scratching his beard. "And all I think of is this: If we *didn't* do it, I would never forgive myself."

"You mean it?" Casey shouted.

Mr. Levin shrugged as if to say, *Would I lie?*

Casey threw her arms around Chip. "I told you!"

"A playwright is born!" Charles exclaimed.

"Mmrf," Chip said, smothered by Casey.

"IS TIME FOR ALL ACTORS TO EAT!" boomed Mr. Michaels from upstairs.

7

April 3, 9:30 P.M.

armchair_holiness: *what was that all about? Bri?*
why did you just hang up the phone on me?

dramakween: u won, ok? im happy for u. harrison-
but u r way too excited about this. don't you dare
ask me things u know I cant do.

armchair_holiness: *u on the rag or something?*

dramakween: i hate that expression. u asked me
if i would DIRECT the show. what did u think i would
do??? carry on a deliteful chat?

armchair_holiness: *it was just a question. i had to*
know. We called our 1st mtg for tmw.

dramakween: & u have heard the answer like 1000
TIMES!!!

dramakween: i am not getting involved. i have sat iis and three ap exams. beside, casey has asked me to give chip a pep talk. she's afraid he'll get cold feet.

dramakween: and out of the deep wellsprings of kindness of my big heart, i said yes. so i talk to chip & that is it 4 me. u direct, harrison.

armchair_holiness: i want to play a role. which means i cant direct.

dramakween: ok, dashiell then.

armchair_holiness: he directed grease. but look i don't want to argue, ok? we'll work it out. we have bigger problems anyway. like the play. the ending sux. i mean, the play is a masterpiece, and then at the end he just goes home.

dramakween: who?

armchair_holiness: win. he gets out of the loony bin and goes home and lives happily ever after. it's the only part of the play that's boring.

dramakween: that's a terrible ending.

armchair_holiness: i know. he has to rewrite it.

dramakween: he's so full of himself. he's going to freak.

armchair_holiness: not if U tell him

dramakween: ME???????

"'Savor the flavor'? 'Them talented youngsters'?" Charles said, emerging from the lunch line with Casey. "Oh, good God. Did you *read* that blog? I thought you said Brett was a writer."

"He was just being ironic," Casey said.

"Clobbered with clichés!" Charles shouted. "Cornered by corniness!"

"When people mention us in blogs, it's usually complaints about casting," Casey said. "This was nice."

"Doll, if Weasels sticks to dirty gossip, rumors, and sex, I have no problem with it. But frankly I get nervous when he drags the DC in."

"Shhh, he's right over there," Casey said, gesturing toward Brett, who was sitting at a table near the window, alone.

But Charles was looking in the other direction. "Will wonders never cease? Brett the Hottie is eating by himself—and meanwhile across the room, if you follow my unobtrusive glance, Chip the Socially Challenged breaks bread with none other than the fabulous socialite Brianna La Glaser . . ."

"She's giving Chip a pep talk," Casey explained, glancing over at the table where Chip and Brianna were locked in intense conversation.

"That's Brianna, always pepful."

"She can't do the show. But her heart is definitely in the Drama Club."

"Yes, and we know where *your* heart is, darling," Charles said, veering toward Brett. "Oh, Bre-ett! Mind if we join you?"

Casey cringed. "Hey," Brett said, turning around with his mouth full of bacon cheeseburger.

Charles set his tray down and pulled out a chair for Casey. "We were just discussing Weasels."

"Coolio. I was just thinking about you," Brett said. "Look what I've been writing."

He leaned forward expectantly, showing Casey his legal pad.

DC UNPLUGGED
• First Original play EVER!!
• RHS Hatches a Genius
• Behind the Scenes
• From Idea to Performance. Heartbreak.
Laughs. Embarrassments. Etc.

"What do you think?" Brett asked. "I got the idea from Casey."

"It's a little more normal than the Weasels," Charles said. "Which brings me to your blog, Mr. Brettastic. I have a few comments—"

"This isn't about the blog," Brett said. "Mom and I were talking, and she was telling me all these stories about people on the board—" He saw the blank look on Charles's face and said, "Sorry. She's on the town board of ed."

Charles sighed. "Of course. Another Ridgeport over-achiever."

"She was giving me the dirt on them," Brett went on. "Some of the board members are real losers. One guy nearly swallowed his false teeth at a meeting . . . anyway, they're all about how many kids go to Harvard and Yale. To them, we're all a bunch of stats. So I started thinking about what Casey suggested, to do a feature article about the DC in the *Rambler*. She's right. You guys deserve more than just reviews. And I don't mean more typical mainstream media crap about money, parents, history, pep rallies. A piece about what *really* goes on. The process."

His face was so earnest. And excited. And Casey had to admit, it *was* a great idea. Brett would love the DC rehearsals. And the DC would love him.

"Interesting," Charles said. "Although I would have to bribe you to keep you from reporting on my use of torture on the Charlettes, in clear violation of the Geneva Convention. Now, just *how* would you research this?"

"I'll sit in on the casting, the rehearsals," Brett said, "get to know everybody . . ."

"We're having a meeting after school today," Casey said eagerly.

"Um, not so fast." Charles folded his hands on the table and took a deep breath. "Hate to be the poopyhead here, kids. And you know I love publicity as much as the next exhibitionista. But there is one teensy problem—the rehearsals are a closed shop. No outsiders."

Casey looked at him oddly. Come to think of it, no one from the outside ever *did* attend rehearsals, but she didn't know there was an official *rule*. "Is that, like, in some rule book?"

Charles nodded. "No one but actors, DC officers, faculty. Our bylaws. Stipulation 13, Clause 3, Subclause C. Actually I made the numbers up, but it exists. And it makes sense, too. Visitors are distracting. It's about freeing the muses of the creative royalty, dahling, so they can make magic, unpressured by outside influence."

"Totally cool," Brett said. "I'll work around it. Actually I haven't even gotten full approval yet. Artie Sprengle has to sign off on the idea. He's the EC. Editor in chief. But we're buds, and I think this is his kind of article."

"Couldn't we just vote on it?" Casey asked Charles.

"Honey, close your eyes and visualize what King Harrison would say about that."

Brett laughed. "As long as you guys think it's a good idea, let me ask Artie, and then we'll take it from there. I will do whatever is best for the DC. Deal?"

Charles smiled at Casey. "He is *such* a nice boy."

8

"CHIP IS DOING WHAT?" CASEY ASKED, GRABBING AN armful of books out of her locker.

"That's impossible!" said Brianna, whose locker was next to Casey's.

Kyle shrugged. "I just talked to the Chipman. In gym. At my locker. I spend a lot of time at my locker now because of the crutches. I go there and listen to tunes 'cause I can't do much else. Sixth period. Anyway, he was all, like, tight and quiet. I was like, 'Hey,' he was like, ''Sup,' I was like, 'Dude.' Just kind of like that—"

"Riveting, Kyle," Brianna said. "Cut to the chase."

"Chip is taking his football away," Kyle said. "Going home. Quitting. That's what he told me. Bye bye, play."

Brianna slammed her locker in disbelief. "I had this

long talk with him at lunch. I told him he was a genius. I told him we were counting on him."

"He says you told him the play sucked," Kyle replied.

Casey's heart sank. Brianna was supposed to have given Chip a pep talk.

"I said the *ending* sucked," Brianna said. "But *sucked*, in fact, was not my word of choice. I said the ending seemed tacked on. Imported from a different kind of play."

"You did?" Casey said. "But you were supposed to be supportive."

"I *was*!" Brianna said. "We are talking about the last few seconds of a long and very supportive conversation, in which I told him that only the *genius* who wrote the rest of the *brilliant* script could possibly revisit the ending and provide another one equal to the rest of the *masterwork*. God, I buttered him up so much I nearly slipped off the chair."

Casey nodded reluctantly. "But Chip is very sensitive—"

"Chip, basically, is an egomaniac," Brianna replied. "Which is why I like him. He fits right in with the DC."

"Dang," Kyle said. "If only I knew. I could have just, like, thrown a football around with him during gym. Then I'd ease him in, like, 'Yo, Chipster, I hear your play's great, et cetera . . .'"

"If you threw a football at him, he'd be in the hospital," Brianna said, pacing the floor. "Where is he? We're about to have a meeting to talk over auditions. Dashiell's working on a poster. He's obsessed with it. All of this is highly inconvenient, considering we no longer have a script."

"Hmm . . . mmm . . ." Kyle grunted, nudging Casey in the ribs and cocking his head to the left.

There was Chip, head down, tooling down the hallway under the weight of his monogrammed L.L. Bean backpack.

"Maybe I should talk to him?" Casey asked.

"Go, tiger," Brianna whispered.

Casey shoved her locker shut. Chip was walking quickly, but she caught up with him by the back door of the school. "Hi!" she called out breezily.

Chip whirled around, barely breaking stride. "Oh. Hi. I'm in a hurry. I have to get home and do some research for debate."

"And . . . the Drama Club meeting . . .?"

"I've taken Brianna's advice," Chip said, barreling toward the door to the parking lot. "I'm reworking the play. It's not ready . . . I'm withdrawing it."

"But Brianna likes the play," Casey said. "She told me."

"Overtly, maybe," Chip said. "But I am skilled at reading the handwriting on the wall. Everyone thinks the play sucks. And upon reflection, they have a point . . ."

"Everyone loves it," Casey argued. "It's just the ending that needs work. Don't withdraw the play, Chip. Please?"

He pushed his way outside, and Casey followed. The air had a surprising bite, and she huddled against the chill of a gathering storm. Chip walked straight for the grove of trees by the edge of the duck pond. He was wearing an open pea coat and no gloves. "Where are you going?" Casey asked.

"A shortcut," Chip said. "As I said, I'm in a hurry."

"Chip, maybe you're overreacting," Casey said.

Chip stopped by an old sycamore tree and whirled around. "Brianna called the ending all wrong. Anticlimactic. Boring. And she's right. That has always been my problem. I can begin things but I have trouble ending them."

"It's only an ending," Casey said. "You can change it, can't you?"

Chip dug his fingers into the tree's peeling bark. "That's the trouble with *fiction*. Fiction is about wishes. It's about how you want things to happen, not about what really happened—" He cut himself off and looked away.

"Really happened?" Casey said, walking closer.

"Never mind," Chip said.

"Chip? Are you saying this story . . . the play . . . is true?"

"No! Yes. Sort of." Chip turned toward the duck pond. A flock of geese landed with an argumentative squabble, then paddled off in separate directions. "I hate talking about this . . ."

"You don't have to if you don't want . . ." Casey said.

Chip nodded. When he began talking again, his words were slow and halting. "Not me. My cousin . . . Justin? God, he was smart and funny. And cool. Older than me. He was, like, perfect. His dad, my uncle, had gone to medical school *and* law school. Then he did this Internet start-up and sold it for a fortune. He pushed Justin, and Justin was expected to do better. But how do you do *better*? Justin was this sweet guy who liked to go fishing and play guitar. So one day, he gets his college acceptances . . ."

"Oh, Chip . . ." Casey put her hand on his arm. "Did something bad happen? Was it like the play?"

He stood still for a long time. Casey couldn't tell if he liked feeling her hand on his arm or resented it. But she kept it there until he spoke again, in a voice barely audible. "He had to go to rehab for a year. I haven't seen him since he got out. He ran away. My aunt and uncle were so upset. His e-mail address went dead. Maybe everything worked out. I don't know. The families lost touch . . ."

Chip was shaking now. She felt his warmth against the cold.

"Don't tell anyone, please," Chip said. "I—I just don't like talking about it."

Casey knew how he felt. She took his hand and sat with him until his breathing became slow and even.

The clock was ticking.

Harrison chewed the top of a pen as he stood in the doorway of the auditorium. At least they'd been able to get the auditorium for this meeting, but after auditions they'd need to dig up a new location. He scanned the rows of seats, then looked into the lobby. Chip was nowhere to be seen. Neither was Casey.

If they were going to do this play, they had to nail an audition schedule *now*. It was April 3, and they had to start rehearsals within a week to make this work. The meeting was supposed to have started ten minutes ago. Chip's tantrum was wasting a lot of time. The Drama Club did not have room for another diva.

Reese was walking in from the school's front door. Brett Masters was with her, carrying a small notebook.

"I tried Casey," said Reese, flipping her cell phone shut, "but I'm still getting her voice mail."

"I say we give them fifteen more minutes," Harrison said. "Then we send out a manhunt."

"Girlhunt," Reese said.

Brett had come to a stop in the lobby. He was leaning against The Wall, RHS's historical shrine of cast photos. He was scribbling in his notebook, the tip of his tongue protruding ever so slightly from the side of his mouth, his hair falling in front of his face.

Brett Masters, Cub Reporter.

"Did you guys look behind the school?" Brett asked. "I can try. If you don't mind me butting in."

Actually, Harrison preferred that to Brett's hanging around the lobby, nosing around. "Sure. See what you can do."

"You bet," said Brett, running off.

Harrison and Reese walked into the auditorium. "I hope he doesn't become a pain in the ass," Harrison said.

"It's a nice ass to have a pain in," Reese said. "Not that yours is so bad."

"Eureka!" Dashiell called out from a seat in the auditorium. He gestured toward his laptop, on which he had been tapping furiously. "Well, ladies and germs, *should* we have this play, I have designed a bodaciously cool audition poster!" Proudly he turned the screen around. "Voilà!"

SCALDING! Seating!

RIPPED FROM THE TRUTH!

Come AUDITION for the Drama Club's

FIRST EVER

UNOFFICIAL

ORIGINAL PLAY!

"Early Decision"

by Chip Duggan

Friday, April 4
3:45-5:30 P.M.
Sides will be provided.

This is NOT a musical.
Those attempting to sing will be prosecuted to the full extent of the law.

Mr. Levin nodded politely. "Well."

"Hmm," said Harrison.

"Uh," said Reese.

Charles peeked over Harrison's shoulder. "Eeek! Who's the face? Lose him, *please*! For his sake and ours."

"He's *Winthrop*," Dashiell protested. "I think he's attitudinally appropriate—"

"He's *scary*," Reese replied. "And maybe delete the joke about the singing? Some people will be offended."

"What does 'ripped from the truth' mean?" Harrison asked.

"I've heard of 'ripped from the headlines,'" Reese said. "And 'based on the truth.'"

"It's Dashiell's phrase of art," Charles volunteered.

"Back to the drawing board, I suppose . . ." Dashiell snapped the laptop shut. "Well, when I *do* get it right, I would like to disseminate it in such a way as to draw in the whole school community. For example, imagine applying the power of Brett's social network, say, to the DC—"

"Dashiell, if Chip doesn't show up, we don't even have a script," Harrison said.

"Exactly," Dashiell said. "Which will be a test of the power and flexibility of new media. In the absence of Chip's script, we could solicit *ideas* through social networks. Create a narrative of our own. A participatory drama. A kind of Wiki-play."

That did it. Harrison grabbed his coat and stood. "Guys, let's wrap it. My bad. I'm a jerk. Mr. Levin was right, there are too many problems doing a play like this. I'm sorry I wasted everybody's time . . ."

As he backed up the aisle, the door to the auditorium smacked open. "Am I too late?" a high-pitched voice rang out.

Reese, who was in the middle of a plié, nearly lost her balance. "*Chip?*"

"Found 'em!" Brett shouted, waving to everybody from the back. "See you all tomorrow."

As Brett left, Chip rushed into the auditorium with Casey close behind. He stood behind the last row of seats. "Ahem. Well. Hi."

Harrison took a deep breath. Chip did not look well. "We're glad to see you, bud," he said. "Do you have something to tell us?"

"Yes." Chip nodded nervously. "I just had a long talk with Casey. I wanted to tell you that *Early Decision* is a thing of the past."

Great. Just great. Harrison flipped his jacket over his shoulder and headed up the aisle. He could barely look at Chip. "Well, thanks for thinking of us."

Reese looked as if she was going to cry. "Oh, Chip . . ."

"It's now *Early Action*," Chip announced.

Harrison stopped. The room fell silent.

"You know, like *Early Decision*, only less binding?" Chip said uncertainly. "Okay, maybe that sucks. But Casey and I had some new plot ideas. I haven't figured out the ending yet, but that will come. I think."

"Chip, wait," Harrison said. "Are you telling us that we're *on* again?"

"Well . . . yes," Chip said.

"WOOOOOO!" Reese raced up to Chip and gave him a kiss. "You are so-o-o-o hot."

"I am?" Chip said.

"Hallelujah," Mr. Levin murmured.

"Wait—title change—let me pull up Photoshop . . ." Dashiell tapped ferociously on his keyboard, the laptop screen facing Chip. "An audition poster, ready to go, per your approval."

Chip's face brightened. "Excellent! That's Win—that's exactly how I picture him."

Dashiell grinned triumphantly.

Harrison sat quietly. He massaged his forehead. He hadn't had a migraine since he was fourteen. A moment ago he'd felt one coming on.

But with each breath, it was now disappearing.

9

Notes for article
Brett Masters

~~There's this old joke~~
You see the DC perform. You know they're good.
The Times says so. The audiences say so. All those
standing O's—you're there, too. But you have this
nagging feeling. It's like that old joke—how many
actors does it take to change a lightbulb? Answer:
500, one to change the bulb and 499 to ask, "How
come I didn't get that part?"

Admit it—most of the time you're like those 499
actors.

I am.

If you see me at intermission, hiding in the hallway, bouncing off the walls and saying "Ow," it's because I'm psychically smacking that little voice inside that says, "I coulda done that!" Okay, okay, yeah, I suck. When I audition, the fleas in the curtains run away. Still, I make excuses: the casting was rigged . . . they weren't listening—but really it's jealousy. I wanna be One of Them. To have all that talent, to get all that applause. The only one who likes my singing is the rubber ducky in the shower stall, who never stops smiling even when everyone else in the house is screaming for me to stop.

So . . . shazzzzzzam! Enter Masterman, the guy who traded acting talent for insatiable curiosity, the man with a mission. To break through the fourth wall and find out the truth behind RHS theater.

Drama Club, unplugged.

Casey liked it. It was rough, a little wordy, but it definitely showed a lot of love and affection for the DC. She looked toward the classroom door. Ms. Ahmed would be coming in any minute. "Nice start," Casey whispered, quickly walking over to Brett's desk to return the sheet of paper.

"Thanks," Brett replied.

As Casey returned to her seat, Chip darted into the room. His hair looked like a sparrow had nested there, and his eyes were bloodshot. Slipping into the seat next to Casey, he whispered, "I rewrote the first act. I stayed up till three-seventeen A.M. It just flowed out. Wrote itself."

"I thought you were going to rewrite the ending," Casey whispered.

Chip nodded. "Our conversation made me think of all different ways to make it better. So I started at the beginning. Totally rewrote that. Put in a party scene—"

"We have to freeze the script," Casey said, "probably before the first rehearsal. It's only fair to the actors."

"We will," Chip said. "But listen—a lot happens in this version. And I bring in another character. A love interest. Someone special who really helps Win. He meets her in the hospital."

"I like it," Casey said.

"Good, because her personality is based on someone I know," Chip said.

"Who?"

"You," Chip said. "And I want you to play her."

Casey laughed so forcefully it came out more like a quack. He had to be kidding. Casting her? In a serious part in a serious play—a starring part? Once upon a time, Brianna had tried to convince Casey she could act. It was just after Casey had moved to Ridgeport, and Brianna had practically forced her to audition for *Godspell*. Casey had done chorus parts in musicals at her old school, but Ridgeport was different. Disaster was not a strong enough word to describe what happened at her audition—the notes that seemed to die in midair, the way her body stiffened like an arthritic turtle. Plus, there was also the issue of what her mother would think if she did the play. This was serious content they were dealing with. "No. Uh . . . no. I can't, Chip."

"For this part, you just have to be yourself."

"I *stage-manage*, Chip. I play piano a little. That's about it. I auditioned for a play once, and I swore I'd never do it again."

Chip pulled a copy of the script out of his bag and set it on her desk. "Just read it. You'll see."

She wanted to shove it right back into his bag, but the pleading look on his face stopped her. That and the fact that Ms. Ahmed was entering the room.

"Augustus?" she said, beaming at Chip. "I saw a sign-up sheet near the auditorium. I see the Drama Club is producing your play."

"Yes," Chip said. "And it's *Chip*."

"That's glorious!" Ms. Ahmed said. "I counted five names already on the list. *Molto* congratulations!"

"Augustus is da bomb," Brett said with a warm smile.

Five?

The number sounded low to Casey, especially so close to the end of the day. Oh well, straight plays weren't as popular as musicals, she figured. It would take a while to catch on.

"Twelve, thirteen, fourteen . . ." Charles said, counting the names on the list outside the auditorium door. "*Fourteen names?* By the end of the day? That's all?"

It was just after last period, and Mr. Levin and the Drama Club had all gathered around. "Was the PA system working this morning?" Casey asked. "Maybe they didn't hear the announcement."

"Dashiell called the play cold," Reese said. "No wonder no one signed up."

"*Culled*," Dashiell corrected her. "I said 'a play culled from the wellspring of Ridgeport's endlessly deep talent pool.' Something vivid to pique people's interest."

"Sure gets my blood going," Charles said with a yawn.

"We have a couple more days," Mr. Levin reminded them, holding open the door to the auditorium. "We'll run the announcement again several times. Let's face it, a student play doesn't have the 'Aha' value of *Rent* or *Pajama Game,* so we have to work a little harder. Shall we?"

As they all filed into the auditorium, Casey glanced back toward Chip. He was lingering at the sign-up sheet, writing something.

Quickly he raced to her side. "You forgot to sign up," he said. "I penciled you in."

"Thanks," Casey replied. She had been planning to do it later. Much later. Like so far near the bottom that maybe they would run out of time and she might not even have the chance to audition.

Harrison was already shuffling papers as she and Chip took seats in the auditorium. "A couple of announcements," Harrison said. "Number one, we'll be able to hold the auditions in the auditorium, but that's it. After that, the place is booked—band and orchestra rehearsals and concerts, a PTA function, blah blah blah. Mr. Levin has agreed to help find another space for us to rehearse. Probably one of the study halls, or the cafeteria. Number two, he is generously allowing us to do a total, one hundred percent student production. By school rules he has to be here, but he's just going to watch. So it's up to us, guys—which leads to number three: staff. Brianna will be sitting this one out. And I'm planning to audition for a role. Which leaves us with three choices for student director."

"Count me out," Reese said.

"As much as I enjoyed my own momentous directorial stint on *Grease*," Dashiell said, "I was hoping to return to the position I know and love, technical services coordinator, or resident geek."

"Casey?" Harrison asked.

"She's auditioning," Chip piped up. "For the role of Maya."

The place fell silent for a moment. Harrison looked uneasily at Charles, and then away. "I guess we could go outside the group . . ."

"And what am I," Charles said, hands on his hips, "chopped liver?"

"Charles? *You?*" Reese cackled. "Oh, God help us . . ."

"Hussy," Charles hissed.

Casey loved the idea. Charles was the one who had brought her back from her disastrous *Godspell* audition. He'd made her laugh and feel comfortable—and he'd welcomed her into his backstage society, where her work made everyone realize she would be a good stage manager. Charles did things like that. He brought out the best in people.

The trouble was, he had never directed.

"Would you want to do it?" Dashiell asked.

"You're needed backstage," Harrison said. "The costumes, the scenery, the makeup, the props—the Charlettes!"

"Yes, granted, that would be a hardship," Charles said. "It would leave them orphaned and helpless, poor things. But I'll be there for consultation. And besides, it's a smaller production, so the demands would be easier."

"I like the idea," Casey piped up.

"Me, too," Dashiell added.

Reese nodded. "I can see it, I have to admit."

Everyone looked at Mr. Levin, who shrugged. "It's your production. But if you want my opinion, I'd say you've got a born leader."

"Harrison?" Dashiell asked. "You agree?"

Harrison sighed. "It will be a steep learning curve."

"I am sure that if I fall off it," Charles said, "you will push me right back up."

10

"WEE-UN? WEE-UN? NAH, PLEASE PUT DOWN THAT bowl, yew know hah exPENsive it was foe yo dadduh an' me . . ." read Sandra McGill in the strangest accent Harrison had ever heard. Sandra's eyes suddenly bugged out, her left hand adhering to her face as if by an unexpected magnetic force. *"Wee-un? AAAAAAGGGGHHHHHH!"*

The scream did it. It redefined loud and ugly. Harrison tried not to cringe. You had to be polite at auditions. People were very sensitive. Besides, Charles was director now. Let him do the reacting.

"Thank you!" Charles blurted out. "That was . . . uh, lovely. Callbacks will be posted tomorrow."

Sandra smiled triumphantly. "Well, just so you know,

I'll have to miss the first Tuesday of rehearsals for a doctor's appointment. Then the second Wednesday is my sister's sweet sixteen, and possibly the third Monday I have an audition for Agapo Opera in New York City. And of course, who knows after that? But I'll be happy to work the rehearsal schedule around your play."

"Uh-huh, great," Charles said. "Thanks for the heads-up. Would you send in the next person, Barry Squires?"

As Sandra walked out, smiling confidently, Reese whispered, "Where did that accent come from?"

"It was supposed to be Southern, I think," Harrison replied.

"More like Martian," Charles said.

From a few rows behind them, Brett Masters let out a chuckle. With Brianna gone, he had helped with sign-up and stayed to watch. He leaned forward and said, "I think she thinks that you already cast her."

"No kidding," Harrison said, turning around. Barry was already bounding down the aisle. "Ssshh."

"Yo!" Barry called out, sounding very much like his character in *Grease*, Kenickie. He was six three and a little heavy, and his hair was streaked with gray.

"Tell me you're reading for Dad, because if you're not, I have some terrible news for you," Charles said.

"Oh. The gray." Barry laughed. "Yup, Dad."

Charles shuffled through a stack of "sides," excerpts from the play. He handed one to Barry. "Let's take the scene after Win has been left at the hospital, where Dad has his little meltdown with Mom."

"Sure," Barry said, quickly scanning the pages and

walking upstage, toward a standing door frame left over from the set of *Grease*.

Harrison leaned over to Charles. "Why are you giving him *that* scene?"

"Because it's his character's big scene," Charles said.

"You *never* give an auditioner a scene where he has to be angry," Harrison patiently explained. "They tend to shout their way through, and it's hard to judge talent."

"Ah. This is news to me . . ."

"Plus, it's a solo scene—no one else onstage. How are we supposed to see how he reacts to others?"

"Well, aren't I just learning by the minute." Charles turned to the stage. "Okay, Barry—whenever you're ready!"

WHACKKK!

Barry slammed the door so hard, the whole frame nearly toppled. Harrison *hated* "angry actor" audition scenes. All the bellowing and screaming. He braced himself.

"Don't . . . talk . . . to me . . . about *pressure!*" Barry said.

Softly.

Almost inaudibly.

This was unusual. Barry's face was red. Deep red. His teeth stood out behind retracted lips as he began pacing the room, moving oddly, as if he were in the dark. As he delivered his lines—his disbelief over Win's breakdown, his suspicion that drugs might be involved, his fear over his son's future, his own guilt—Harrison felt a chill. Barry delivered his last line—"I've lost a son"—squatting in the corner, arm holding on to the back of his head as if keeping it in place, his voice tear-choked and distorted with emotion.

Charles was frozen, staring. Brett, just behind him, was scribbling furiously on a legal pad.

Barry finally stood up and shrugged. "Um, that's the end of the scene."

"Oh!" Charles replied. "Can you just stay there and do the whole play—all the parts?"

"Charles is kidding," Harrison said. "Callbacks will be posted tomorrow. Thanks."

As Barry left, Charles hissed, "You stole my line. About callbacks."

"You didn't say it fast enough," Harrison said.

"What am I doing wrong?" Charles asked. "You're acting like I'm doing everything wrong. Like the scene choice. It wasn't bad after all—it ended up being great!"

"The bit about him doing all the parts," Harrison explained. "You never tip your hand to the actor. Stay impartial."

"It was a *joke*," Charles said.

"Even a joke. You know how it is. Actors take these things to heart." Harrison checked the sign-up sheet. "Casey?" he called out.

"I'm supposed to call out the names, too!" Charles said, snatching the sheet back from Harrison.

From the back of the auditorium came a rustle of hushed voices. Harrison turned to see Chip gesturing to someone in the auditorium-door alcove. Slowly Casey stepped out from the alcove, with a wan smile. "Hi," she said, walking down the aisle.

"I'll read the part of Win," said Chip, following behind her. "Casey is auditioning for Maya."

Charles arched an eyebrow.

Harrison held tight to his pen. He hoped this would be short and relatively painless. Casey was an amazing stage manager, but her audition for *Godspell* had been, well, an unfortunate experience.

"This scene takes place at Gowanus Hospital," Chip said. "Win has been there for a week. He's talking again. But he's high on Xstasy, given to him by another kid there—Kayla, a sociopath who deals drugs secretly."

Chip, as Win, pretended to open a door. He stumbled to center stage, with an odd expression that made him look like a dazed chimpanzee.

Harrison tried to concentrate on Casey. This was *Casey's* audition.

Standing stiffly on stage left, she said, "I don't think I'm supposed to be here."

"Who cares?" Chip said. "Goddamn Nazis run this place. What do they think we're gonna do?"

Casey walked in tentatively. She looked around the room curiously, pantomimed picking up a photo. "Is this you?"

"Maybe." Chip pretended he was reaching under a mattress for drugs.

"You look different . . ." Casey's face changed. A look of shocked recognition. "Hey. I know you. "

Chip spun around, hiding something behind his back. "You *know* me?"

Casey moved closer. "Are you *on* something, Winthrop?"

"What makes you say that?" Chip asked.

"What's in your hand?"

"None of your business."

Casey lunged forward, and Chip fell back, releasing the hand he had been holding behind his back. "Look what you made me do!"

"Dr. Stone?" Casey called out, recoiling, looking terrified.

"Don't do that!" Chip shouted, scrambling to his feet. *"Don't do that or I'll kill you!"*

"Dr. Stone!" Casey shrieked, running offstage.

Chip stood stiffly and turned to the front. "That's the end of the scene."

She was good, Harrison thought. He quickly scribbled on his evaluation sheet:

Charles bolted out of his seat, applauding. "Bravo! Bravissimo! Darlin', where did *that* come from? Didn't know you had it in you!"

Casey was grinning. And why wouldn't she be? Charles had nearly told her she got the part.

One . . . two . . . three . . . Harrison tried to be calm, smiling as impassively as he could.

"Great, Casey—thanks!" Charles called out. "You know the drill. If we decide to call you back, blah blah blah . . ."

"She'll be there!" said Chip as he and Casey walked offstage.

"Charles . . ." Harrison murmured.

"I know, I know, I tipped my hand," Charles said softly. "But it's *Casey*. And she was wonderful, and don't tell me you didn't agree. Anyway, what happened to Ms. Meltdown from *Godspell?*"

"I guess the singing made her nervous," Harrison replied. "Her acting's pretty good."

"You realize," Charles whispered as Casey and Chip walked toward the back of the auditorium, "if we cast her, we have yet another crisis."

"Which is . . . ?" Harrison asked.

"Who's going to be our stage manager?"

The migraine was back.

11

"I THINK I'LL SAY NO," CAME CASEY'S VOICE OVER the phone.

Brianna couldn't believe what she was hearing. "Wait. Did they offer you the part already?"

"No, but they're going to," Casey replied. "Charles told me."

Brianna burst out laughing and flopped down on her bed. Quickly she noted the time. She was in the middle of a practice test for an SAT II, but it could wait. She would suspend timing for this. "Casey. That is so great. You must have blown the doors off. You will not say no. This role was written for you. By your boyfriend."

"He's not—well, I don't really know what we—"

"Okay. Your whatever. For now. Until Brett realizes what he's missing."

"Brett?" Casey asked.

"We're drifting off topic," Brianna said. "I know, I know, you're loyal to Chip. Yawn. But the point is—don't be an idiot. Say yes to this great role."

"But I'm the stage manager," Casey protested. "That's what I do."

Brianna waved her hand dismissively, as if Casey could see it. "Get someone else to do it."

"Who?"

"It doesn't matter, Casey! Find someone. You're not using the main stage, right? I thought Levin booked up the lecture hall. How complicated can it be?"

"It's harder than you think," Casey said. "The SM plays nanny to everyone during rehearsals . . ."

"It's a small show, Casey. They can nanny themselves."

"And work out the lighting with Dashiell . . ."

"Lecture hall. It'll be low-tech."

"Have you ever worked with Dashiell?"

Brianna let out a little scream. "Casey! I will *not* let you talk me out of this."

"Talk you out of what?"

"Talking you into this! Look, the SM for this show wouldn't even have to come in until tech week. God, *I* could do it."

"You could?"

"No sweat."

"What about SAT IIs? Those would stop you. Lots of people are taking those."

"Tech week is afterward. It wouldn't be a problem."

"Really?"

"Totally."

"Brianna, that is so cool. I love you so so so much!"

"That's why I'm here on this earth," Brianna said with a smile, glancing over toward her suspended practice test.

"I can't wait to tell Harrison and Charles!"

"Give them a wet kiss from—" Brianna suddenly sat up. "Wait. Tell them *what*?"

"That you're going to SM!"

"I—I didn't—"

"'Bye!"

Click.

As the line went dead, Brianna stared at the phone. She immediately tapped out Casey's number.

Voice mail.

With a sigh, she flopped down on the bed. If she called and made a stink, they would be back to square one. Casey refusing to take the role.

What had she done?

She took a deep breath. Actually, the idea didn't seem so bad. Not if she could avoid all the pressure.

Tech week, she told herself, putting down the phone.

It'll only be tech week.

RIDGEPORT DRAMA CLUB
FINAL CAST LIST, *EARLY ACTION*
Student Director, Charles Scopetta
Stage Manager, Brianna Glaser
Faculty Adviser, Mr. Gregory Levin

** First rehearsal, Thursday, April 10, Room 132 **
** Performance, May 30, TO BE DETERMINED **

Winthrop . . . . Harrison Michaels
Dad . . . . Barry Squires
Mom . . . . Jenny Koh
Maya . . . . Casey Chang

Patients (and Kids at Party):
Kayla . . . . Shara Simmons
Jack . . . . Hassan Baig
Rob . . . . Dino Testaverde
Chloe . . . . Deena Mallory
T-Cell . . . . Randy Schwartz
Frank . . . . Royce Reardon
André . . . . Jason Goldstein
Taki 245 . . . . Antoine Pauling

Part 2
Room 132

April 10

12

"PEOPLE! PEOPLE! LET'S TAKE IT FROM THE TOP!"
Charles called out.

Casey jumped from her seat in back of Room 132, the
larger of the two study halls at Ridgeport. She was jumping
a lot these days. And doing many other undesirable things.
Like overeating. And not sleeping.

And worrying, worrying, worrying.

I'm going to suck.

The thought had hardwired itself into her brain as
a fact. An incontrovertible truth that would pop up at
any given time. When she was going to bed, when she
was eating dinner or talking on the phone or IMing or
studying—*suck suck suck suck*—there it was.

Especially when she was memorizing lines, which

was just about all the time. All day long she could barely concentrate in class. Everything seemed like a line from the play.

What had she gotten herself into?

It was all because of Chip.

He had talked her into this. She never should have said yes. She never believed *the DC* would say yes—to casting her in anything. Let alone as a *lead*!

Casey squirmed in her seat, a cramped wooden chair with an attached desk, encrusted with hardened gum and carved with the message D.K. + PYTHO 1994, rubbed over the years to a blurry dullness. Just like her mood.

Everyone else was all excited. The leads in Act One, Scene One, were walking to a big staging area in the front of the room where the teacher's desk had been pushed aside. Barry, Jenny, Hassan, Shara, Dino, Deena, Royce— they all seemed so psyched and happy.

Other people *liked* to act.

This was *not* how she planned to end her junior year, being miserable, scared, and pessimistic. Things had been going so well. *Why couldn't she have left well enough alone?*

"Hey, are you okay?" came Harrison's voice, from her left.

A cue. She knew that line . . . "Um . . . Fine, Winthrop, but you look lousy."

Harrison burst out laughing. "God, you are nervous. That was me, Harrison, speaking. I really meant it."

Casey felt herself turning red. "Sorry."

"Casey, this is a rehearsal," he said, taking her hand.

"We're all in the same boat. It's okay to be nervous. It's okay to make mistakes. That's what rehearsals are for."

Casey nodded. She took a deep breath and looked around the room. Brianna was smiling warmly at her. It felt so good to see her there. Brianna had agreed to show up today, for this first rehearsal, to calm Casey down. After today, Brianna wasn't coming back until tech week.

That would suck. Why did Brianna have to be so busy? Who was Casey going to turn to?

Why did everything seem so miserable?

"Let's take it from the top, kids—opening tableau!" Charles said. He was wearing glasses with narrow frames and leafing through a large artist portfolio pad with drawings.

"Hey, no worries," Harrison said. As he ran up to the staging area, the door opened and Chip walked in.

Chip looked as horrible as Casey felt. "Oh, dear, it's Christopher Walken on a bad hair day," Charles murmured.

"Couldn't get the ending right," Chip said, handing Charles a stack of papers. "I know we have to freeze it soon, but I want to work on the last act a bit more. Am I fired?"

"Of course not. We're not going to get anywhere near the ending today," Charles replied, and then shouted, "Charlettes, please distribute!"

Vijay Rajput, the new head of props and costumes, took the stack. "We are no longer the Charlettes," he said. "We are now the Rajputians."

"Do Rajputians have arms and legs, or must I place

these scripts upon the top of their winged exoskeletons?" Charles asked, then turned to the rest of the room. "People! Please take the scripts, courtesy of Chip, who has clearly been working his butt off for us.

"Okay—for our rewritten opener, let's have a split-screen effect, very moody, very cinematic—on stage left Win at a school party, hip-hop blaring, a huge prism ball reflecting light into the audience—well, a small one, if we can find it. On stage right, an empty suburban living room. Mom and Dad emerge onstage through the front door, home late from work, the power couple. Dad turns the light on. Mom has the mail and looks crazy-excited. She drops the mail on the floor except one envelope—the thick college acceptance. At the same time, stage left, while the other kids dance, Win holds a drink, *trying* to have a good time. But he's shaking. Slightly. Trying to keep it under control. Panic-stricken. We don't know why. *He* doesn't know. Claustrophobia? As he backs away, tripping over people, desperate to get out, Mom opens the letter—and she and Dad begin to jump up and down, like kids. Two sides of the stage, two scenarios. Neither side aware of the other. Oh! Very *dramatique, n'est-ce pas?*"

"I get *verklempt* just thinking about it," said Vijay drily.

From the back of the room, Dashiell said, "I don't recall ever receiving these lighting directions from you!"

"I just made them up," Charles replied.

Casey laughed. She wished she had what Charles had. He never got nervous. Even in a new job. What a refreshing change from the other student directors—the efficient but moody Brianna, the technically brilliant but forgetful Dashiell.

"Stage left, party scene, let's go!" Charles said. As the actors in the scene scurried into place, the rest of the cast and DC officers sat back silently. Suddenly a familiar tune blared out of a boom box at the back of the room—the overture to the Broadway musical *Carousel*.

"CUT!" Charles called out. "What is *that?*"

With a *click*, the music stopped. "Sorry," Dashiell answered, "I didn't know which CD was in the player. I'll hook up my iPod to the input jacks."

"I'm imagining a Jay-Z vibe here," Charles said.

"Got it," Dashiell said. Almost instantly the right music began, and everyone but Harrison started dancing. Harrison was alternately smoldering and looking desperate, pacing the stage as if he were a trapped animal.

"This is not Greek tragedy here, Harrison," Charles called out. "Subtle, subtle, subtle."

Harrison's face tightened. "Thank you."

On stage right the door opened and Barry and Jenny bounded in.

"Guys, you are *parents!*" Charles shouted. "You are too frisky. It has been a long day at work. Will you please *sag?*" He leaped onto the stage and pressed Barry's shoulders down. "I know you're supposed to be happy, but not *kid* happy. *Parent* happy. Everything a little softer and slower. Let's take it from the top of the scene."

Dashiell played the track again. Harrison stood

stockstill, looking pasty and uncomfortable. Definitely an improvement, Casey thought. But on stage right as Jenny came through the door, she looked as if she were underwater, walking stiffly and making weird faces.

"Cut!" Charles cried out, his head in his hands. "*Cut!*"

Harrison was tapping his foot impatiently. And Casey wondered if they would ever get past Scene One.

"Hey, Casey, wait up!"

Casey turned to see Brett trotting up behind her. She was headed out the door, chatting with Chip. Well, *listening* to Chip was more like it. The rehearsal had been rocky for everyone. She had managed to do her scenes and say her lines, which under the circumstances was a major triumph. But now Chip seemed to need a reaction to every single comma he had written.

"Hi, Brett," she said.

"How'd it go?" Brett asked.

"Fine," Casey said.

"Lousy," Chip said.

"Which one, fine or lousy?" Brett asked.

"Charles is great," Casey said.

Chip shook his head. "He's trying too hard."

"The actors are still learning," Casey said.

"No one knows what they're doing," Chip said.

"It depends on how you look at it," Casey said.

"Wow." Brett laughed. "Sounds like you need an outside observer."

Casey nodded. "Maybe you could sit in on the next rehearsal."

"What about the rules? I thought rehearsals were a closed shop," Chip said. "Actors and staff."

"I'm sure no one would mind," Casey replied. "It's a win-win. Brett helps us, we give him material for his article."

"Fine with me," Brett said with a shrug. He pushed open the front door, holding it for them both. The sweet, cool aroma of spring wafted in. "You guys want a ride? I have my car."

"I get sick if I write in cars," Chip said, bounding away. "See you tomorrow."

He was a fast walker, writing in his notebook without breaking stride.

"Genius," Brett said.

They were alone. Leaving the school, walking toward the only car parked in the lot, alone. Her and Brett.

This felt strange. Why did it feel strange? They were just walking. Still, she felt like she was splitting into two, herself and another Casey hovering, watching. There was a piece of conversation in the air, her hover-self reminded her. It was Casey's turn. All of a sudden making conversation felt like a very complicated affair.

"Einstein was a genius," she mumbled.

Minus ten points for stupid.

Brett pointed his remote key chain at the red Corvette in the lot. "Ride?"

"Okay," Casey said. "Thanks."

As they walked toward the car, the silence felt oppressive. She thought about an article she had read in the local paper about auto safety. "I read somewhere that red cars are in more accidents than any other color."

Oh God, that was dumb.

"I'll get you there alive," Brett said, opening the passenger door for her.

"So formal," she said nervously.

Maybe she should just shut her mouth and when necessary grunt directions. After that whole switch-up with the plays, Brett had to hate her by now, and no doubt would be happy if she just refused to get in.

As she sank into the passenger seat, he shut the door behind her, then ran around the car and slid into the front seat. "I like to be formal. I grew up watching old movies. My dad does the best Jimmy Stewart impression and I do Cary Grant."

"Uh-huh," Casey said. Her hands were trembling. *Trembling.* "Um, how does it go?"

"What? The Cary Grant?" Brett turned the ignition. "I barely know you."

He pulled away from the curb, his tires squealing.

Casey's stomach lurched. She grabbed the armrest. Was this the Cary Grant imitation? Did he do racing movies?

"Sorry. I just got this car last week. I'm still getting used to it," Brett said. "Let's see, bad driver, too formal, bad taste in colors . . . what a loser, huh? I guess you're trapped."

Casey exhaled. Counted slowly to ten. Unclasped her fingers. Stole a look at Brett. He was smiling. Hover-Casey was looking around at the world, screaming *He doesn't hate you! He's in the car with you and SMILING!*

"Where to?" he asked.

"Um, Yale Drive," Casey said. "Please."

Brett laughed. "Harvard Avenue, Yale Drive, Princeton Street, Dartmouth Road—do you think they do it on purpose? Like, what parent wouldn't want to live on Harvard? They figure it'll rub off on their kids."

"Hmm? Oh. Maybe."

Talk much, Case?

He flipped on the radio. WINS. *The Sandy Kenyon Entertainment Report.*

As he reached for the controls, Yale Drive appeared. Brett pulled his arm back to the steering wheel and made the turn. Sandy was reviewing *Das Schauspiel,* which he called "a period comedy about a traveling theater group in Germany that will make you laugh so hard you'll fall off your *sitzplatz.*"

"Hey, that's the film I was telling you about," Brett said. "Have you seen it?"

"Not yet," Casey said.

"I hate subtitles," Brett said, pulling to the front of her house. "But it's playing around here—I'll go if you go with me."

Casey shrugged. "Sure."

"Maybe this weekend," Brett said.

"Okay." Casey let herself out of the car and leaned in to wave good-bye. "Thanks!"

"Later!" Brett said.

As he drove down the block, a lot faster than he'd been driving, Hover-Casey returned to her body, and they both thought the same thing at the same time.

Oh. My. God.

13

"ARE YOU SURE?" BRIANNA SAID OVER THE PHONE.

Casey adjusted her headset, pacing her bedroom. "He asked if I saw it. I said no. And he said we should go. This weekend."

"And you said yes, right?" came Brianna's voice.

"I don't know! I think I did. But I was like a zombie. I wasn't even expecting the ride home. I was saying stupid things. I don't even know what was coming out of my mouth."

"'Yes.' Please say you said yes. Recover this memory, Casey."

"What is *wrong* with me?" Casey said. "What if I did say yes? Is it a date? What if Chip finds out?"

"Oh, for God's sake, you're not eloping. It's a movie with subtitles. Think of it as a reading."

"But Chip would never . . . I mean, he trusts me," Casey said.

"Are you madly in love with Chip?" Brianna asked.

"It would really hurt his feelings—"

"What about your feelings? You can't just be thinking of his. He'll just take advantage if you do that. And you didn't answer my question."

"Well, I'm not *madly in love*, no, but we're not really *dating* dating. He hasn't even really asked me out yet and—"

"So go out with Brett. It may not mean anything. Look, Casey, he's a guy. Guys fall asleep at subtitles. He knows you'll pay attention. He just wants you there to fill him in."

"You think?"

"Definitely," Brianna said. "And then, afterward, you'll have sex."

"Brianna, will you be serious?" The phone beeped in the middle of her sentence. "Hang on, I'll be right back." Casey pressed the flash button. "Hello?"

"Hey, Casey, 'sup." Chip's voice.

"Hang on a minute." Flash. "Brianna? It's Chip. Gotta go."

Brianna laughed. "A triangle. I'm so proud of you."

"Later." Flash. "Chip? What's up?"

"I'm stuck," Chip said. "In the play. I've been trying to work on it, but avoiding it. With homework. Can you believe it? I'm procrastinating on the play by doing homework! Also TV. And research for the debate tournament on Saturday. It's the ending. I can't figure it out. Win has a breakdown, Win is hospitalized, Win is saved by Maya, end of play. Something else has to happen."

Casey wasn't ready for this. "I . . . I don't know, Chip. I mean, *how would I know?*"

"Casey?" Chip's voice was softer now, concerned. "Are you all right?"

"Fine. Just a little tired. From the rehearsal. Plus I have homework."

Chip fell silent for a while, and then said, "Chubby Hubby."

"*What?*"

"And Phish Food. That's what you need. Ben & Jerry's. I'm bringing them over now."

"But—"

"I know, I know. So do a little homework now, while you're waiting. But think about how I should end the play, and get ready for some restorative ice cream. It'll help both of us."

"Chip, no, you don't need to—"
Click.

April 10, 6:47 P.M.
armchair_holiness: *hey, bri, did the rehearsal seem a little weird?*
dramakween: i don't know, harrison. i was doing homework a lot of the time. 1st rehearsals always suck. why?
armchair_holiness: *it's charles.*
dramakween: i thought he had some good ideas.

armchair_holiness: *about the furniture and the window treatments.*

dramakween: i love the split-screen thing.

armchair_holiness: *it's all about the LOOK.*

dramakween: u want it to look bad?

armchair_holiness: *what about motivation? coaching the actors on line readings? the deeper meanings in the play? the dramatic arc?*

dramakween: im not supposed to be involved.

armchair_holiness: *ur not. i'm just asking a question.*

dramakween: i just spent a half hour on the phone with casey. look, everything is gonna work out. give charles a chance. ur being too greek, stubborn boy. go sleep it off. ☺

14

"OF COURSE THEY DO," REESE SAID, TAKING HER Jamba Juice from the counter. "Everybody sleeps with everybody in the Drama Club."

"No kidding?" Brett said, paying for his juice and hers. "Everybody?"

He was so earnest. Reese was glad she had run into him at the mall tonight. She liked guys like Brett. The package was perfect. Not only earnest but hot-looking. He took everything you said so seriously.

"Why do you think everyone wants to join?" Reese asked, heading for a table that had just been vacated.

"I thought it was about the drama," Brett said.

There it was. That spark in the eye. He had to know it was a joke.

"It *is*," Reese said, waggling her eyebrows. "Nothing but drama, if you know what I mean."

"A double entendre," he said.

"I'm not as dumb as I look," Reese replied.

Brett laughed. "And I'm not as smart as I look."

"You weren't supposed to say that."

"Jesus. Okay, okay . . . you don't look dumb at all, Reese," Brett said with a laugh. "Not close, actually."

"Keep going . . ." Reese said, taking a good hard sip. "And I'll give you all the dirt you'll ever need for your article."

She couldn't believe it. He was taking out a *digital recorder* from his pocket. "The more detail, the better," Brett said. "Sprengle is smelling a Woodward and Bernstein smash."

"Who is smelling a what?"

"Artie Sprengle? He's the *Rambler* editor in chief. He's crazy ambitious and thinks he's some kind of high school newspaper impresario or something. He wants all of us on staff to be these investigative reporters—you know, Woodward and Bernstein, the guys who broke the Watergate scandal in the seventies? Sprengle wants something killer, something prestigious. He wants it bad, for his college app—you know how it is." Brett shrugged. "He's going to want something really in-depth. The juicier the better. Anyway, no one has ever done this. You know, find out what the famous RHS Drama Club is really like. Behind the scenes and all." He held the recorder to his mouth. "Testing, testing."

"Well . . ." Reese leaned closer. "For *some* of the details, I'll have to swear you to secrecy. Lest I have to kill you."

"Deal. Just say 'off the record' whenever necessary."

"Let me put it this way," she said, moving her seat right up next to him. "One of our traditions is, never look in a shadow. Mainly because certain shadowed areas of the stage are reserved for . . . you know . . ."

"Oh . . ."

"There's a freshman corner and a sophomore corner."

"Wow . . ."

"And the Green Room? In the back of the stage? You know why it has a waiting list . . ."

"Really?"

"Clothing optional."

Reese smiled to herself. This was evil. So evil.

15

CHIP'S FINGERS FLEW ACROSS THE KEYBOARD OF Casey's computer. "They're called batch files," he said. "Watch."

Sitting on her bed, Casey watched patiently and ate another spoonful of Chubby Hubby ice cream. It went down smooth and cool, too good to guilt out about.

Her monitor popped to life with windows and lines of impenetrable stuff. "That's code, right?" she asked.

Chip nodded. "Although the Windows operating system, with XP, officially severed its command-line-based structure, it is still tied to the DOS prompt and allows you to create simple batch-file programs in MS-DOS which can be easily dumped, via shortcuts, into your Start Menu—which when activated can be run at the command line in minimized and therefore invisible windows, effectively customizing your computer for functions such as targeted backups."

"Oh," said Casey, trying to sound like she understood anything past the word *although*.

He dragged a file from a folder to the lower-left portion of Casey's screen. Her Start Menu popped up along the left side, and the folder embedded itself. "Voilà! With one keystroke you will now be able to back up all your documents to a flash drive, provided it is labeled as Drive F, which it naturally should be, according to the tree structure. You have a flash drive, right?"

"Right." Where it *was*, she had no idea. Probably at the bottom of a desk drawer collecting spiderwebs and ant turds. "Thanks, Chip. That's, uh, very useful."

"It's my good deed for the day." Chip turned and smiled. "How's the ice cream?"

"I feel much better. Thanks."

"I almost brought Karamel Sutra."

"Really?"

He flinched. "Because it tastes good. Not for any furtive . . . ulterior . . . I mean—"

His glasses slipped down his nose, and as he reached to push them up he sniffed twice and crinkled his nose. That habit again. It meant he was back to feeling cutely nervous. Sniff, sniff, crinkle.

Where had she seen that recently . . .?

"Samantha!" she said. "On *Bewitched—Nick at Nite*? She does that."

"Does what?" Chip asked.

"That thing you do with your nose, when you're nervous."

"I'm not..." Chip's face was turning red, and he realized it. His protest faded and his mouth slowly turned up at the corners.

Then he did the crinkle again.

Casey burst out laughing. He could be such a geek sometimes. But he was here. With ice cream. All because he had heard something in her tone of voice over the phone. Kindness always got to her.

Brett wouldn't have done that. And Brett didn't crinkle.

Why was she thinking of Brett?

She dug a spoon deep into the open container of Phish Food. There was a little left. All the way at the bottom.

April 10, 8:54 P.M.
SCOPASCETIC: *bri, i have dish.*
dramakween: ooh. do tell, herr direktor.
SCOPASCETIC: *masterman and la reese. together at the mall.*
dramakween: reese???????
SCOPASCETIC: *oh, pleeeze. do not tell me ur surprised.*
dramakween: i had no idea.
SCOPASCETIC: *guess brettie is a part of our lives now. hes practically hanging at rehearsals, & u know what happens w boyz (who look like that!!) when our little reesy is around . . .*
dramakween: it's a boy-toy thing. gotta be. she is SUCH a slut.

SCOPASCETIC: *now now, a little envious? maybe ul have to come to rehearsals more often, hmmm? jealous jealous jealous jealous jealous jealous*

dramakween: u have got me SO wrong.

SCOPASCETIC: *wont be the first time. so. aren't ya gonna ask y i was at the mall?*

dramakween: no.

SCOPASCETIC: *i'll tell you. i found wigs. for jenny and barry.*

dramakween: wigs? what happened to silver hairspray?

SCOPASCETIC: *SO old school, darling. i picked up some vintage clothes too. and some curtains.*

dramakween: wait. i thought vj was supposed to do that. ur the director.

SCOPASCETIC: *honey, if your minions arent doing their job, you have to do it yourself.*

He hadn't touched her.

It was her first thought when the houselights went up in the movie theater after *Das Schauspiel* ended. Okay, Brett had brushed his hand against hers a couple of times. But even that was kind of friendly, brotherly. Which was fine. Casey didn't know what she would have done if he *had* tried anything else. She had been so focused on the position of his arm, and the meaning of his body language, and the places in the movie where he seemed bored, that she couldn't concentrate. When he started dozing off, she was sure it was her fault. Which made no sense. Brianna had warned her that guys fell asleep over subtitles. Somehow Brianna knew that.

The fact that he was here, with Casey, made no sense anyway. Brianna had *also* told her about Charles seeing Brett with Reese at the mall. That news had hurt a little but also came as a relief. So why didn't Brett ask *Reese* to the movie? Actually, it would be just fine if Brett were interested in Reese. That would make life less complicated for Casey. She had watched them closely during Friday's rehearsal. She didn't see sparks fly, but it was hard to tell. Sparks weren't flying here, either. At least not from him to her. Maybe this movie was just meant as a friend–friend thing. Maybe Casey just seemed to him like the German-art-film type.

Judging from this crowd, though, the German-art-film type mostly had gray hair and glasses. *Das Schauspiel* did seem well acted and funny. The other people in the theater were laughing. But it was hard to read subtitles when you were preoccupied. Just when Casey would relax into it, she would start to feel guilty. About not paying attention to Brett. About how Chip would feel if he saw her there. About the idea that he might indeed actually *be* there. Sitting behind them. Shocked. Heartbroken and angry.

"So, what did you think?" Brett had asked when they were walking out.

"Um . . ." was about as far as she got before Brett began chiming in with his opinions. Brianna had been wrong. He had paid attention to the whole thing.

They picked up some sodas, and Brett drove to the Seacleft Canal in southern Ridgeport. Along one side of the canal were clubs and seafood restaurants, along the other quiet houses with boat docks. In between was a short walkway with benches and an old wooden railing.

The moon was almost full tonight, and it cast a yellow brick road straight down the canal. From the restaurants' open patios came a din of conversations and music. Casey stopped and took a deep breath of the sea air, briny and thick.

"It's not much different, is it?" Brett said, looking out to sea. "The theater, I mean. All over the world. The people in the movie were just like the DC—the closeness, the personalities."

Casey laughed. "We don't speak German. And we don't have sex all the time."

"I'm not sure I believe *that*," Brett said with a lopsided smile.

Of course he would say that, Casey thought. He had been talking to Reese. "I guess it depends who you've been talking to. Theater people exaggerate."

Brett nodded. "I know. I saw Reese at the mall the other day. She was telling me all kinds of stories. Didn't believe most of them. It's hard to tell with her."

He was honest. Casey liked that.

"Reese is great," she said. "She calls herself our dancer slut. But that's Reese. She likes to give off the image."

"So it's really an act?"

"Sort of." Casey felt uncomfortable talking about people behind their backs. "She's not here to defend herself, you know."

Brett laughed. "True. But you're a good defender for

her. I don't really believe those stories anyway. Her and Harrison in the Green Room. Her and Kyle on a park bench . . ."

Casey felt the hairs on the back of her neck stand up. How much had Reese told him? "Look, when you do a musical, things get really intense. Everyone gets close. It's all really physical. So yeah, you're alone with someone in the Green Room, rehearsing whatever and . . . stuff happens. Reese and Harrison, Reese and Kyle, Brianna and Harrison, Brianna and Kyle, Dashiell and Shara . . . even me and—"

She cut herself off. She had already gone too far. She took a sip of her soda. Brett was looking at her intently.

"You are so lucky," he said.

"It's really about the work, though," Casey insisted. "I don't mean to make it sound like— Not all the—"

"I know. I get that. But all that closeness. Those friendships? I don't have that. Newspaper people aren't like that." Brett shrugged. "I really don't have too many close buds, Casey. I'm kind of jealous."

Casey couldn't help being surprised by this confession. Brett never ever seemed like the kind of guy who would be jealous of anyone. Or lonely for friends.

Suddenly he reached into his pocket and pulled out a coin. "Make a wish."

"I will if you will," Casey said.

"Deal."

As Brett tossed the coin out to sea, Casey decided quick.

"What did you wish?" Casey asked.

"That you won't think I'm a total loser for not knowing anything about theater," Brett replied.

Casey laughed. "That's easy, I won't!"

"And your wish?" he asked.

"That I won't totally make a fool of myself as Maya."

"Wish granted. You'll be swell, you'll be great."

"That's from *Gypsy*," Casey said with a smile.

"It is? See, the Wizard granted my wish, too."

For a long time they both leaned over the railing, their shoulders touching. Along the canal, the restaurant lights were beginning to flicker off, and the tinkle of silverware and glassware echoed off the glassy water.

Casey leaned closer to Brett. She thought about Chip and felt a pang of guilt. But she was cold, and there was nothing wrong with finding warmth.

That's all it was, warmth.

She let Brett put his arm around her, and they watched as a small family of ducks paddled silently into the bright yellow road, veering south toward the moon.

16

April 16, 11:17 P.M.

dramakween: *just because i opted out of rehearsals doesnt mean u can neglect my need for dish.*

dramakween: *u never told me what happened sat night w brett.*

changchangchang: it was awful.

dramakween: *the movie?*

changchangchang: the whole night.

dramakween: *uh-oh*

changchangchang: we went to the canal. we had a long talk. he put his arm around me.

dramakween: *then he dumped u?*

changchangchang: no. that's it.

dramakween: *what was the awful part????*

changchangchang: chip.

dramakween: chip showed up????

changchangchang: no, i mean, what if chip finds out?

dramakween: uh.

dramakween: you're joking.

changchangchang: no! i feel so guilty.

dramakween: wait. u saw a movie. u talked. u had a good time, i presume. but it was awful. what am i missing?

changchangchang: it's awful in retrospect. it started being awful afterward. when i came to my senses. what if brett wants . . . more?

dramakween: u say "OKAY"!!!!!!!!!!

dramakween: or u tell him about your sexy & available friend brianna glaser.

changchangchang: seriously, brianna . . .

dramakween: i am serious. don't worry. play it by ear. these things work out. i know a lot of people who would love to have your problem.

changchangchang: i hate being popular.

changchangchang: am i just weird?

dramakween: yes.

dramakween: which is why i love u.

Playing Win was grueling. Compared to this, Harrison thought, Danny Zuko was a piece of cake. He paced the "stage" area of Room 132, visualizing himself in Win's hospital room, in Win's clothing. In Win's mind. And that's where his imagination failed.

How did you play a person who wasn't a person? Someone who realized that he had crushed his real self. That his soul was dead. That he had never expressed who *he* was, only what other people wanted — perfection. Harrison didn't know anybody like that. Brianna was the closest to the need-for-perfection part. But she was full of personality.

Today they were doing Act One, Scene Seven. The last of Win's "flat" scenes. After this one, Win gets jumped by a few kids in the hospital who don't like him. At least Harrison could show a little emotion there.

Charles poked his head in from the hallway. "People, don't wait for me — go right ahead with the scene. I need to put out a fire with the Charlettes."

Harrison wished Charles would stay put. But he had to give Charles the benefit of the doubt. Directing wasn't easy.

He glanced at his script then stared out the window of Room 132. Jenny, playing Mom, pantomimed opening a door. "Hi, sweetie. How are you feeling?"

"Fine," Harrison said softly, his voice flat, giving her only a quick, guilty look. *Too much emotion. Give her nothing.*

Jenny sat on the edge of the bed. "I guess you needed this, huh? A rest, some good sleep. You know, needing a good night's sleep is the root of so many problems. Most kids wouldn't have to come here if only . . ."

"Mom, can I show you something?" Slowly Harrison rolled up his pant leg. When the makeup people got done with him, his calves would be crisscrossed with scars.

Jenny jumped back. Her brow furrowed, her face turning into a mask of anger. "Oh . . . OH MY GOD, WIN!"

Harrison dropped his script to his side. "Jen, I don't think you're supposed to be angry here."

"I'm not angry, I'm shocked," Jenny replied. "This is my shocked face."

Harrison nodded patiently. Jenny had her own ideas about acting. She made faces. She exaggerated. The more familiar she got with the script, the worse she did. He wanted so badly to take her aside and coach her. But it wasn't his job. He wasn't the director. Charles was.

Where *was* Charles?

Harrison looked around. In the back of the room, Casey was quietly running lines with Reese. Mr. Levin was sitting off to the side, being unobtrusive, grading papers. Dashiell was putting together strings of theatrical lights. The other actors were waiting patiently, doing homework, passing around puzzles. Brianna was home today.

"Haaaaaaa-hahaha!"

A familiar-sounding cackle echoed from the hallway.

"I'll be right back," Harrison said. He scurried out of the room.

A long sheet of white butcher paper had been laid out on the floor, with a big sketch of a living-room set. Charles was poised over it, charcoal pencil in hand. The entire team of Charlettes was there with him, along with Brett—and they were all looking at Vijay.

"Charles, *Charles*, uch, what am I gonna do with you?" Vijay chirped in a high-pitched voice. He was wearing an unscrewed rope mop over his head like a wig. "Clean the schmutz off those fingers, you're a schlemiel like my husband!"

He put his arm roughly around Brett, who was shaking his head, fighting back a laugh.

Brrruuppp, burped another of the Charlettes, Gabe Hirsch, waddling around the hallway in a fat suit and a male gray wig—with Deena Mallory, one of the actresses, hanging on his arm.

"Um, Charles?" Harrison said. "Can you come in here and help us?"

"Can't you see I'm busy at the asylum?" Charles asked. "I have Vijay in drag, and a DC actress so in love she doesn't even care that her boyfriend is a pig."

"Oink," said Gabe.

"He's stupid, but cute," Deena explained.

Harrison didn't want to shout. But they had been rehearsing for a week now, and Charles had spent more time backstage than onstage. "Well, um, Jenny and I are out there on our own," he said, "with no director."

"Darlin', you and Jenny rock," Charles replied. "I am *not* worried about you two. However, out here in the place Where the Wild Things Are, we are having some unfortunate design problems with the Charlettes—"

"Rajputians," said Dan Winston, one of the backstage crew.

"Oh, my wounded pride," mumbled Charles.

"Hey, Vijay's da man now," Gabe said.

"The boss," Deena agreed.

"I beg your pardon," said Vijay, suddenly a soprano again.

Enough. Harrison had had enough. "Uh, *hello?* Charles, do I have to spell it out? You're the *director,* damn it! And Deena, you are in this show!"

He didn't mean to shout, but his voice echoed off the tiled walls. Vijay's eyes bugged. Gabe turned around. The other Rajputians looked up curiously.

As Brett stepped politely aside, Deena quickly slipped back into Room 132.

Charles's eyebrows were in forklift mode, rising high enough to obliterate his forehead. "I do *not* need to be reminded—"

Harrison groaned. "Come on, Charles. *You're not supposed to be back here,* okay? A director doesn't spend all his time playing with props and costumes. A director *directs!* If you didn't want the job, you shouldn't have taken it!"

Charles put down his charcoal pencil. "Finish these drawings as per instructions, will you, Gabe?"

"Sure, Charles," Gabe said.

As Charles turned toward Room 132, he cocked his head toward Brett. "Having fun yet?"

But Brett didn't look up from his notebook. He was writing furiously.

17

CHARLES WAS NOT RATTLED.

Oh, no no no. Being upset would be too easy. Harrison *wanted* that. He was loaded for bear this evening. Or centaur. Or whatever the Greek hunters hunted.

Fizz. Fun. Forward thinking. Those were Charles's watchwords.

As Charles walked into the room, he smiled and waved cheerily to the gathered throng. "Everybody miss me? Don't all answer at once. Let's go ahead to Scene Eight at the hospital cafeteria. Maya and Win."

Casey, who was sitting with Chip, got up and walked toward the stage. She looked funny today. Like she wanted to cry.

Harrison sauntered to center stage. "Where do we stand?" he asked.

"On your feet, darlin'," Charles said.

Oops. Had to keep control of Mr. Temper. "Just a little joke! I would like Win to enter from . . . stage right."

Harrison moved to stage right. "What's my motivation?"

"Well, you're at the hospital trying to get better, and Jack the dealer managed to sell you drugs while no one was looking, and you see Maya—"

"That's not a motivation," Harrison snapped. "Those are circumstances."

"Ah. So . . . well, what do *you* think your motivation is?"

"Motivation, Charles," said Harrison as if he were talking to a slightly slow first grader, "is what the character *wants*. It is the basic thing that *every* actor has to think about."

Keep a lid.

One . . . two . . . three . . .

Too late. Charles's right arm slapped the script down on the seat beside him with a sharp *thwack*. "Would you like a motivation? Here's a motivation. Enter from stage right and do the scene because I said so *and I'm the director*."

"YEEAHHH!" shouted Royce Reardon from the back of the room.

"Charles—?" Casey said.

"Kids, are we having a problem?" Mr. Levin called out, standing up from his seat.

"I think we need a little time out," Charles chirped. "Actors, for the next few minutes run your lines with Chip, will you, while I coach Harrison and Casey in the hallway?"

He gestured for Harrison and Casey to follow and

walked through the open door. He did not stop walking until he reached the end of the hallway, near a side exit. "I am sorry," he hissed. "But do not get me angry, Harrison, because I am not pretty when I'm angry. I say things I do not mean to say. I am trying my best for God, country, and Ridgeport. If you would like to be student director, Harrison, fine, I can live with that—"

"No, I want *you* to be director," Harrison shot back.

"You're a good director," Casey added helpfully.

"Then treat me like a director," Charles said.

"I will, if you act like one," Harrison said. "You have to give up the Charlettes, Charles. You can't do everything."

Charles took a deep breath. "Okay. Okay. One of my obsessive little habits. I will join Charlettes Anonymous. I apologize. But in the future, if you think I'm doing something wrong, please tell me in private. Like now, before we go back inside."

"Okay," Harrison said thoughtfully. "Mark up your script in advance. That will save time."

That was not what Charles had expected. *You're doing a fine job* would have been nice. Or even *I'm sorry, too.*

But Charles was a lover, not a fighter. And Harrison was sometimes a little hard to love, but that was life. "Well, I *have* marked it up," he said.

"With dramatic beats and character arcs?" Harrison asked.

"Well, yes," Charles said. "More or less. But I will do more if you think—"

"Great," Harrison said. "Show it to me by tomorrow."

"What?" Charles said.

It was a joke. It had to be a joke.

"We can't waste time," Harrison said.

It wasn't a joke.

"You are giving me a deadline?" Charles asked. "To write it down?"

"Deadlines are useful," Harrison replied. "So write it all down in the margins and show it to me."

Charles saw nasty little red creatures with goatees and pitchforks dancing before his eyes. He flipped to a new page in his legal pad. "Write it down . . ."

"Can we go back now?" Casey said nervously.

Harrison sighed. "Charles is the director. Ask him. He can do anything he wants."

"Anything?" Charles said.

"That's your job description," Harrison said. "Your mission. Anything to make the play as good as it can be."

"Okay then, how about this?" Charles ripped off his sheet of paper and turned it toward Harrison to show what he'd written.

YOU'RE FIRED.

Masterman0326: ru ok?

SCOPASCETIC: brett—sweet of you to ask. no.

Masterman0326: i overheard everything.

SCOPASCETIC: i know. fun fun fun, huh? life in the dc.

SCOPASCETIC: btw im all for freedom of expression,

freedom of press, and the right to dress up like batman, especially on mondays, but could u possibly not put this in ur blog?

Masterman0326: im keeping this out of the blog. i just wanted to tell u i think ur doing a good job.

Masterman0326: from what i've seen, i mean. which isn't much.

Masterman0326: but u have talent. its obvious.

SCOPASCETIC: thanks. we could use you at rehearsals. everyone needs a little moral support!

Masterman0326: anytime. i mean, i know people are touchy.

Masterman0326: about strangers attending rehearsals.

SCOPASCETIC: darlin, im the director. despite hm's former delusions of grandeur. but he's gone now. & as far as im concerned, ur no stranger, ur one of the family.

Masterman0326: hey, thanks.

SCOPASCETIC: im getting a call from my shrink. this will be a while. i'll be expectin 2 see u tmw.

18

"HE *FIRED* HIM?" BRIANNA SAID INTO THE PHONE. "You have got to be kidding."

Casey was nearly hysterical. Hardly putting sentences together. "It's . . . everything is going wrong. I called Charles, and he . . . he says, 'It's either him or me, and it's not going to be me.'"

"God, those two are birds of a feather," Brianna said.

"And Chip is . . ." Casey said. "I think he suspects . . . me and Brett—but even if he doesn't, he knows I was in the hallway when Charles blew up. Now his play is . . . He thinks I could have played peacemaker. I just know it. And Brett . . . he was there. At the end of the hall, watching. He heard the whole thing. What's he going to write about . . . oh, Brianna, this is a disaster! *What are we going to do?*"

"Casey, are you lying down?" Brianna asked. "Because if you're not, you should be. This is not worth all the angst."

"Okay," came Casey's voice. "Brianna, what if Harrison and Charles never talk to each other again? What if the Drama Club just falls apart?"

Downstairs the doorbell rang, and Brianna looked at her watch: 7:59. "Casey, I think Harrison's here. He said he was coming over to talk at eight, and he's never late. I guess I know what he wants to talk about. Let me see what I can do. I'll call you back, okay? In the meantime, take a deep breath. What's the worst that could happen? Don't answer that."

Brianna hung up. She heard footsteps on the spiral staircase and, a second later, a sharp knock on her door.

She quickly pulled it open, and Harrison bounded in.

"Great, Harrison. Just great," she said. "I stay away from one week of rehearsals, and everything falls apart."

Harrison flopped down on Brianna's bed, trying to look casual and unconcerned. "Hey, why not just cut to the chase?"

"Ha ha," Brianna said. "I found out from Casey. She's all upset. How could you do that?"

"I didn't do anything. He *fired* me!" Harrison replied.

"Because you were trying to control him," Brianna said.

"How do you know?"

"I know *you*. You never think *anybody* can do things as well as you can."

"They'll get someone else to play Win," Harrison said. "I can use the time."

"This play was *your* idea!" Brianna rubbed her forehead, trying to massage away the fact that she had four hours of homework ahead of her and the most stubborn human being on the planet standing in her way. "Do you know how unprofessional this is?"

"Not my fault—"

"You did this to the DC once already. In *Grease*."

"That was totally different—"

"You got the part. You gave us rehearsal time, just enough time to show how good you were. And then you left us."

"But that wasn't my fault, either!"

"It never is. It's always someone else. Your dad. Charles. They stand in your way and prevent you from being right! And you? Do you ever compromise? Do you ever back off and count to ten? Do you try to consider the other person's point of view? Their feelings? No! Why should you? They're wrong and you're right!"

"Exactly."

Brianna slowly leaned over, banging her head against the pile of papers on her desk. "I don't know why I am friends with you."

"Must be because of the hot sex and good food."

"One for two ain't bad." Brianna wished she hadn't said that. Her relationship with Harrison . . . that was definitely not a topic she wanted to get into tonight. "Don't change the subject," she told him.

"*You* did!" Harrison howled. "Look, what am I supposed to do, go begging to Charles for my job back—in the play that never would have existed without me?"

Brianna looked up. "Well . . . if you did, he might take you back."

"Ohhhhhhh, no," Harrison said. "I will not go there."

"Do you *want* to be in the show, Harrison?"

"*Yes—but I was fired!*"

Brianna took a deep breath. *Drop it*, she told herself. This was exactly the kind of thing she had wanted to avoid. They had already dragged her into this play up to her ankles. Harrison was *not* going to pull her into the undertow.

"You do whatever you want, Harrison," she said, turning to her screen and trying as hard as she could to focus on the Taft-Hartley Act and tomorrow's history quiz. "Don't let the door smack your butt on the way out."

She felt her cell phone vibrate and quickly glanced at the screen. Charles. When was it ever going to end? She waited for Harrison to leave then wearily flipped open the phone.

In the den of the Scopetta house as the clock struck 10 P.M., seven candles glowed on the coffee table. A CD Charles had found in his dad's collection, called *Classical Vistas*, was playing softly in the background. Around the table, sitting cross-legged and crowded, were the officers of the DC and major members of the cast: Brianna, Casey, Reese, Dashiell, Shara, Barry, Jenny, Chip, Hassan Baig, Vijay, Dino Testaverde, and Royce Reardon. Despite the fact that Charles had provided enough milk, ice cream, M&M's, and chocolate-chunk cookies (baked with loving dedication by himself and his mom) to feed three Drama Clubs, everyone looked slightly uncomfortable.

"Welcome to the Charles Scopetta group therapy session, based on an idea by Dr. Eustis Fink," Charles said.

"Dr. Fink told you to burn candles and serve cookies?" Hassan asked.

"And play terrible music?" Dino added.

"We are here to channel support and niceness, Dino dear," Charles said. "The candles were my idea. For that mystical, magical something. Don't worry. I'm not going to make you hold hands and sing 'Kumbaya.' I would simply like to talk about my favorite topic. Me."

"And why you're such a schmuck," Vijay added.

"Thank you for that," Charles said. "Okay, true confessions: this afternoon I kicked Harrison Michaels out of the show. He was being a real . . . oh, keep me from wicked words . . ."

"Putz?" said Vijay.

"Thank you, Vijay, I'm confident you will nail the Yiddish Insults AP exam," Charles replied. "Now, we all know Harrison, Mr. Volcanic Moods, his good and bad points. And we all deal with him in our own way. So, I have been asking myself ever since — was I an idiot or was I justified?"

"Are we taking a vote?" Barry asked. "I say idiot."

"Schlemazel," Vijay interjected.

"Gesundheit," Dino said.

"I say justified," Jenny piped up.

"You were rough on him," said Reese.

"He was rough on Charles," Hassan pointed out.

Charles listened carefully as a spirited debate arose, definitely tilted in Harrison's favor. "I will take this under advisement," he said. "Question Number Two: Can we do this play without him?"

"No way," said Jenny.

"Absolutely," said Barry.

"Can we change the music?" Reese asked, looking slightly nauseated.

Dino threw an M&M at her.

Charles felt his head sinking downward, with the sinking realization that Dr. Fink should have his license taken away. They were all fidgety and giggling, like preschoolers. "Uh, people?" he called out, clapping his hands like Mrs. Cromarty at Ridgeport Montessori School.

A flying chocolate-chip cookie nearly hit his nose.

"Damn it, knock it off!" he shouted, rising to his feet. "Kids, I did not *want* to be director. I did not *ask* for it. I am making mistakes, big time. And when I make too many mistakes, I say, oops, Charlesie, you are in over your head. And I bail. Let me tell you, campers, I'm *this* close—and if I bail, the play is over."

Quietly Dino began picking up cookie crumbs from the carpet. "Sorry," he said.

The others shifted in uncomfortable silence as Casey calmly leaned forward. "Charles, I have a question. Did you really mean to kick Harrison out?"

"At the time, yes," Charles said.

"Do you *want* Harrison in the play?"

Charles took a deep breath and sat back down. "Do you?"

Dashiell nodded. "Picking a new Winthrop will set us back a few days. We can't afford it."

"Besides, nobody is as good as he is," said Royce.

"Then we have a problem," Brianna said. "The ego. When you kick out Harrison, he stays out. We've seen this happen before. He's stubborn."

Reese was now fiddling with the stereo system, and a Coldplay CD began. The others were staring at one another, staring at Charles.

This was knotty. If he asked himself, during the brightest of moods, *Am I mad at Harrison?*, the answer was always yes. Mad about his piggy behavior. About the absence of "I'm sorry" from his vocabulary.

Charles drummed his fingers on the coffee table. It all boiled down to ego. Harrison's and his own. The two elephants in the room. One of them would have to step aside.

And sometimes, when you were the leader, you had to.

He stared at the coffee table, deep in thought. A dish of M&M's had been knocked over, colored candies spilling across the wood. Dino took a handful and shoved them into his mouth.

In a moment, Charles knew just what to do.

19

HARRISON HATED THE LATE SHIFT, BUT LATE SHIFTS were a fact of life in the diner business.

Niko the 24/7 waiter was not made of steel. He had to be sick once in a while. When he was, Harrison's dad always knew where to turn, especially now that Harrison would have a little more free time on his hands than he had planned.

"*Haralambos!*" Mr. Michaels boomed, barreling out of the kitchen with a glare that did not lose its intensity as he greeted customers along the way. "Ah, hello, Mr. Rodriguez, how's you mother? Jimmy, nice to see you! Mrs. Bloom, you like the stuffed green peppers? *Haralambos, why you no serve Table Nineteen?*"

Harrison wiped a wet cloth over Table Four, picking

up the last of three globs of hardened chocolate syrup left by the Padroonian family triplets. "Dad, could you *please* call me Harrison in public?"

His father let out a deep sigh, which had the heft and sound of a hydraulic brake. Everything about him was outsized—from a voice always verging on a shout, to the number of framed photos of himself on the diner walls, to the gut that despite grueling eighty-hour work weeks still lapped lavishly over his size-40 black leather belt. "Okay, okay, *Harrison* . . . why you no serve Table Nineteen?"

"It's not my station," Harrison explained. "I have Tables One through Eight. But if you *want* me to go there and leave this mess to someone else, hey, done deal . . ."

"I clean," Mr. Michaels said, reaching for Harrison's wet cloth, "and you serve Table Nineteen!"

Taking his pencil from behind his ear, Harrison headed for the other side of the diner, glancing at the chalkboard menu for specials. He ran them quickly in his mind— *Yankee bean soup, Manhattan clam chowder, shrimps with orzo, giouvetsi lamb stew.* Table Nineteen was a long banquette in the back, a high-backed booth just inside the el that led to the restrooms. It would be a pain to take all those orders, but a big party meant big tips. "Hello," he said, turning the corner into the booth of Table Nineteen without looking up, "my name is Harrison and I'll be your waiter for—"

"*Surprise!*"

Harrison nearly dropped his order pad. There, crowded around a table for eight, were Charles, Brianna, Casey, Reese, Dashiell, Shara, Barry, Jenny, Chip, Hassan, Vijay,

Dino, and Royce. In the center of the table was the famous specialty of the house, Kostas Korner Kitchen Sink—thirty scoops of ice cream, five toppings, and whipped cream, on a bed of split bananas and chewy brownie.

Charles pulled back his chair and stood. Grabbing an empty ice-cream bowl in two hands, he knelt and bowed his head low, raising the bowl as if it were the Holy Grail. "Harrison, on behalf of the officers and actors of the Drama Club, who have been unwitting and unwilling, um . . ."

"Recipients," Casey whispered.

"*Recipients* of a hissy fit between two stubborn idiots—namely, you and *moi*," Charles said, "I bring you this peace offering of forgiveness and light."

"*Etsi, bravo!*" boomed his dad's voice from behind him. Harrison turned. Dimitri the waiter was there, too—and George the chef, Despina the cashier, and a couple of curious customers.

"You *planned* this . . ." Harrison said.

"And you'd better say yes, fast," Charles said, "'cause my knees hurt."

Everyone at the table laughed. They were all grinning with anticipation.

No, Harrison thought.

This was too easy. Too . . . *Drama Club*. The Big Scene. The Happy Reversal. The next part of the script was the Smiling Reconciliation.

"But—" Harrison began.

"You sit, Tsarles," his father called out. "You, too, Haralambos. Is slow tonight. You sit with friends. Dimitri take you tables until you finish."

"But we have a problem here," Harrison said. "It's between me and Charles. It's a management problem, and it's not fixed so easily—"

"*Vre* Haralambos, you no manager—you *kid!*"

"Dad, this doesn't involve you!"

"*You sit down—or you fired!*" his father bellowed.

"I've already been fired," Harrison shot back.

"*Then you fired twice!*" Mr. Michaels retorted.

They were standing face-to-face, nostrils flaring.

"My God, they're twins," Jenny said.

That did it. Harrison felt the blip in his chest, which turned into a choked-back hiccup, which diverted to his nostrils and came out as the most badly concealed (and ugliest) laugh of the century.

"HAAAA!" roared Mr. Michaels, instantly turning red.

"Oh, good Lord, hallelujah, they're friends again," Charles said, struggling to his feet. "Let's eat."

Harrison sighed, pulled aside a chair, and girded himself against thirteen pairs of lunging arms.

20

"HOLD IT!" CHARLES SHOUTED, WALKING TOWARD the staging area. "Jack—that was a good scene, but why are you being like that?"

"Like what?" said Hassan, who was playing Jack, a kid at the hospital who gets into a fight with Win.

Charles winced. They could talk like normal people in real life, why couldn't they do it from a script? "Talking in that high-pitched voice, all singsongy," he explained.

"I'm being earnest," Hassan said. "That's what it says in the script. It says, 'Jack, open bracket, *earnestly*, end bracket.'"

"Ah, okay," Charles said patiently. "Think about this: I know that a director must be patient. So do I say to myself, 'Act patiently to Hassan'? No. I say, 'I need to help Hassan make the scene come to life.' That gives me a constructive goal. And the goal is what makes me patient." Ooh. That sounded good. Charles was impressed with himself. He cast a side glance at Harrison, who was smiling.

"Um, it says 'earnestly,' not 'patiently,'" Hassan reminded him.

"*I'm using an example!*" Charles said. "Sorry. A person is earnest for a reason. What is your reason?"

"Um . . . well, I'm seeing that Win is a mild guy, kind of weak," Hassan said. "I want to sell him some drugs and make sure he doesn't rat me out."

"Yes!" Charles said. "*That's* what you keep in mind— all the time. *What do I want?* That's your reason, your motivation, your *objective*. If you do that, the earnestness will come. And it'll be the right kind of earnestness— *sneaky* earnestness. Now let's take it from the top."

Turning to go back to his seat, Charles clutched his dog-eared script, which had been marked up in the margins. Today, all day long, between classes and during, Charles had studied it—plus an e-mail Harrison had sent after midnight, discussing his views of the play. It had printed out to four pages, single-spaced.

"How'd I do?" he whispered to Harrison.

"Perfect," Harrison said.

"I have a few text questions for our genius writer," Charles said. "Where is he?"

Harrison shrugged. "Still sleeping off the Kostas Korner Kitchen Sink?"

Charles smiled. From the hallway, he could hear Vijay and the Charlettes—er, Rajputians—discussing furniture with Mr. Ippolito, the custodian. On "stage," Hassan was pacing, trying to get into his character. Royce and Jason, playing other kids in the hospital, were making up elaborate frat handshakes.

"Knock-knock-knock," Royce said, pantomiming a knock on a door. "Yo, Vijay, are we going to have a door here?"

"Gevalt! Whaddaya want, we're barely a week into rehearsals!" came Vijay's voice from the hall.

"Translation: yes," Charles said.

Royce buried his face in his script, reading his opening line: "'Sup, Jack?"

"Motivation, Royce," Charles demanded. "*Motivation!*"

"Um, I'm scared of Jack, but I also want to score some?" Royce said.

"Go for it."

Royce kind of slithered across stage. "''Sup, Jack?'" he said in a tentative, cagey voice.

"Oh, good Lord," Charles said, leaning into Harrison, "the air is thick with acting."

I am suffering the curse of the Black Plague.

Casey fought to pay attention to traffic as she biked to Chip's house. The conversation on the cell had been horrible. He had sounded so depressed, so hopeless. She could barely understand what he was saying . . . and then, the Black Plague? It had to be a joke. Or an exaggeration.

But Chip hadn't been at rehearsal today. He had

seemed out of it lately. Maybe something really was wrong with him.

People didn't still get the Black Plague. Did they?

She dumped her bike on his lawn and ran to the front door. It was open. As she ran through the house Chip's parents were nowhere to be seen. A boiled-over pot sat on the stove, an open box of cereal on a counter.

"Chip?" Casey called out.

No answer.

Chip's thirteen-year-old sister, Rumer, poked her head out of the den. She pointed tentatively upstairs and then disappeared back in.

Casey took the steps, two by two, and found Chip at his bedroom desk, his blinds drawn, the light of one lamp illuminating his desk as he sat slumped over his keyboard.

"Chip?" Casey said. "How are you feeling?"

Chip sighed, not even looking at her. "Not great."

"Is there anything I can do?"

"Give me a brain transplant," Chip replied.

Casey pulled up a footstool that had been propped against the wall.

"I'm so close," Chip said. "I get Win out of the hospital. Everyone thinks he's okay. But it's like, a false climax. He's developed a drug addiction. Everything falls apart. So far so good. But how do I end it? He dies? He gets rescued in a violent gang fight by the docks? Nothing works."

"Endings are hard . . ." Casey said, even though it was about the lamest thing she could think of.

"And the worst thing is, I've been working on it so

hard I have allowed my debate scores to suffer. One of the judges gave me a five last weekend at CFL. A *five!* That's out of six. One is best. I always get ones, twos, and threes . . ."

"Well, it's, um, no use getting sick over it," Casey said.

"The goddamn blank page!" Chip said, gesturing at the monitor. "It's a curse."

"Wait—blank page?" Casey laughed. "Is *that* what you were saying?"

Chip turned from the computer, blinking, as if he had just now noticed that Casey was there. "Hmm?"

"Over the phone," Casey said. "The *curse of the blank page?* I thought you said *Black Plague!*"

"You thought I had the Black Plague?" Chip's eyes widened.

"The cell connection was bad."

"That's why you came so fast?"

"Well, not really . . . I mean, I didn't really *believe* . . ."

"Haaaaa! Oh, that's great. That's amazing. Hooohoohoo." He nearly fell off his chair laughing. Hiccuping with laughter.

It wasn't *that* funny. "Stop it!" Casey said, reaching out to give him a smack.

He put out his hand to stop her. His fingers closed around her wrist. Casey pulled back playfully but he held fast. He wasn't laughing anymore.

He pulled her toward him, pulling her off the footstool. She was kneeling on the floor now, looking up at him. He wasn't letting go, but there was nothing forceful about the grip. Slowly, he moved toward her, and all the while she was thinking this couldn't be happening—but it was and she was enjoying it all, the brightness of his eyes, the smile that said she'd managed to help him out of a mood, the grip that he probably never used with anyone else before.

And as he drew nearer, on an instinct she closed her eyes. The air between their faces went suddenly warm. And she felt the press of his lips, softer than she expected, sweet, with a sad, salty tang.

21

CHIP CLOSED HIS EYES. SHE WAS GONE, BUT HE could still smell her. A jasmine-y kind of scent, probably not perfume or anything, just soap. Shower gel. Whatever.

"What happened?" said Rumer, poking her head into his bedroom.

"Nothing," Chip replied.

"Did you do it with her?" she asked.

"Did I *what*?"

"Do it?"

"Do you even know what that means?"

"Do you?"

Chip picked up Claude the Crab, the only Beanie Baby he still had left over from childhood days, and threw it at her.

Rumer ran away, squealing, and slammed the door behind her.

As her steps pounded down the stairwell, Chip sat up. He could taste Casey's lips still. Not a food taste, not anything identifiably sweet or sour. Like his lip molecules had been altered but were slowly reverting to their original state, leaving only a vague sense of regret.

Sense by sense. Smell, taste, touch. His fingertips. The pores of his skin. Everything felt different. Unclogged. Open. As he looked out the window, the path to the front door seemed outlined in charcoal pencil, sharper-edged. And the soft chords of an Iron & Wine tune breathed barely audible through his speakers, as if chosen for this moment.

He stood up and turned to his computer. It was time to get back to work.

His monitor flashed its screen-saver slide show, random photos from his collection—Rumer at the beach, buried in sand up to her chest; Mom at her company's Concert for Work/Life Balance, singing along. Chip sat at his desk and reached for the mouse.

His hand stopped in midair.

There he was. Cousin Justin. Maybe eleven years old, on the beach in Nantucket, smiling right into the camera, next to an enormous sand sculpture of a blue whale. Or maybe a humpback, only Justin seemed to know the difference—but it was a recognizable whale, as opposed to the hideous shapeless lump being built by Chip. Justin looked as though he had just stepped out of the water, all fresh and clean, while Chip was sunburned and encrusted with sand, working too hard to notice the camera. That's the way it always seemed to be. Justin was older and wiser and smoother; he wore sunscreen and his skin never peeled; he was able to make magic with sand and papier-mâché and even a stick of charcoal.

The image vanished, flickering to the next. Chip shook his mouse, took a deep breath, and clicked on his document.

End of Act Two. Blank page.

The Black Plague.

He smiled. And he began typing.

Early Action
© Augustus "Chip" Duggan, 4/18
Act Two, Scene Twelve

22

"YOU GET JUMPED," CHIP SAID.

Casey sat forward expectantly. It was Saturday. Chip had asked for a weekend rehearsal, then asked her and Harrison to meet him early in Room 132, before the other cast members came.

"Jumped . . ." Harrison wrote furiously in his notebook. Harrison kept an actor's notebook—every possible detail about his character. "Who jumps me?"

"Jack," Chip replied. "Your nemesis from the hospital. He was let out at the same time. He fooled them. They think he's done with violent behavior. But he teamed up with Kayla, the dealer at the hospital. They picked up a few customers there. Kids with money. Including you. Jack and Kayla can't wait to do business."

Harrison looked up. "So why would Jack jump Win? He turned Win into an addict. You don't attack your customers."

"Because, at the end of Act Two, Win shows up at a meeting place and refuses to buy. He wants to go clean. Maya has helped him figure this out. She's helped him realize he hasn't ever expressed his own desires, his own self. Just before this, they have a big scene. I wrote a killer monologue for Win."

"Ah . . ." Harrison said, writing again.

"Anyway, in the middle of the fight, Maya shows up . . ." Chip's voice was soft, faraway-sounding. "She gets in the way. She gets hurt. A cop siren sounds. Jack and his friends run. Win holds Maya. They rock back and forth. He's worried about her. Crying. He apologizes. He is just learning to express emotions. To express who *he* is. It's all because of Maya—and now this. It hurts more than he can bear—but he lets it all out. She's badly hurt. He's scared of losing her. Of failing. Then the cops come. His mom and dad are with them . . ."

His voice trailed off.

"Uh-huh," Harrison said. "And then?"

Chip shrugged. "Maya's eyes open. They see each other. Their eyes connect. The lights fade."

"That's *it*?" Casey said.

"What's the resolution?" Harrison asked.

Chip looked at him curiously. "That *is* the resolution. Maya is going to live. Win is whole again. He's a person. He has his own desires and goals. But he's going to have to build his life from scratch."

"Does he say that?" Harrison asked.

"The audience will feel it," Chip said. "Not everything has to be tied up in a bow."

Harrison exhaled. He grabbed a script and headed for the hallway. "Okay, let's go with it. I'm going to get a soda. Either of you want one?"

Casey and Chip shook their heads.

The room fell silent.

Casey smiled at Chip. "I like it," she said.

"It's the happy ending I wanted," said Chip, in the saddest voice Casey had ever heard.

She put her arm around him as the Drama Club began filing in.

"Deena?" Charles called out. "Deena Mallory!"

According to Charles's schedule, it was time for the big hospital good-bye scene, when Win is released. One of his hospital friends was played by Deena. Who had been grafted to Gabe's side for most of the rehearsal process.

Where *was* she?

Charles looked around Room 132. Chip was in the back, slumped in a seat, looking like his eyes were about to close. Casey was sitting next to him, eating a candy bar and urging him to take a bite. Harrison was fine-tuning his acting in the corner. Brett was laughing about something with Reese.

"Take five, kids," Charles said, "while I find Miss Deena and pluck her from the cauldron of desire."

He darted out into the hallway. Today Vijay and the others had moved their operations into the auditorium's backstage area, because the hallway had become too small for their ambitions.

Charles jogged to the doorway marked STAGE LEFT and yanked it open. "Helloooo! Has anyone seen darling delinquent Deena?"

At the same time, all four of the Rajputians bolted to their feet and chirped, "Nope!"

"Well, *that's* convincing." Charles eyed the costume-room door, which was closed.

As he walked toward it, Vijay stepped in front of him. "I'll find her."

"No worries, I have a nose for this," Charles said. He barged past Vijay and flung open the door. "I'm not *look*-ing . . . but you have five seconds!"

From the dimly lit room came Gabe's voice. "Huh?"

Charles heard a rush of frantic noise from the area of the old sofa, last used in a production of *Pajama Game* but obviously still functional. "Hi, Charles," Deena said, sidling past him, her makeup smeared.

"I don't know how the Rajputians work," Charles said, looking in toward Gabe, "but the Charlettes had a strict rule against snogging the talent during rehearsal. We do *not* need added melodrama in this production. Play on your own time, but on my time, *you're working!*"

They were both out the door before he finished, elbowing their way through a clutch of people who had gathered at the doorway.

On his way out, Charles brushed by Brett. "Welcome to the world of the theater, doll," he said.

23

"I'M SORRY, DASHIELL. AS YOU KNOW, I CAN'T COME to a Drama Club meeting now," Brianna said, pulling a lightweight jacket from her locker.

Dashiell stood fidgeting behind her, as always, with his arm around Shara. It was odd seeing them in this section of the school at the end of the day. Brianna didn't even know where Dashiell's locker was. She had a feeling he didn't either. "Have you checked your in-box today?" he asked.

"No, but I'll see any messages when I get home," Brianna said. She threw on her jacket, tossed her hair over the collar, and shut the locker door. She was *not going* to get involved.

"Well, um, there's important news," Shara said.

"I'm all ears," Brianna replied, "but for a limited time only."

Dashiell and Shara followed her down the hallway. "Three things," Dashiell said. "One, Mr. Levin was able to get us the use of the cafeteria for the performance. We'll perform the show against the north wall, which has no windows. We'll curtain off part of the hallway as a backstage. Two, our opening date has changed."

"Opening?" Bri echoed. "I thought we only had one night, May thirtieth."

"That's the news," Dashiell explained. "We can do the show twice, but it has to be Thursday, May twenty-ninth, and Saturday, May thirty-first. The cafeteria is being used Friday for the Ridgeport Seniors Yoga-lates Class. Don't ask."

"Well, that'll all work. What's the third thing?"

"Look at this." Dashiell fumbled in his pocket, looking left and right. "But hurry or I'll be caught. Cover me, Shara."

He held out a BlackBerry. Dashiell was the only student at Ridgeport High who had a BlackBerry.

Brianna squinted at the tiny screen:

From: <rhsseniorclasscommittee@rport.li.com>
To: <recipient list suppressed>
Sent: Tuesday, April 22, 10:35 A.M.
Subject: HARBOR FESTIVAL, MEET SHAWN NOLAN
Hi! Your senior class has some great news! Come to the waterfront for the four-day Annual Harbor Festival. Not only do you get great ethnic foods

(including FREE souvlaki from Kostas Korner), but on the kickoff night of the festival, Thursday, meet TV star SHAWN NOLAN, who will be starring in a Long Island summer-stock production this summer!!!!

When: Thursday, May 29, 7 P.M.

Where: Starts at Duke Ellington Boulevard, from Rendell to Harbor

Why: Why not?

"Cool," Brianna said, without breaking stride. "He's in my locker."

Dashiell looked dismayed. "Shawn Nolan?"

"A picture of him," Brianna replied. "He used to do musicals, you know. As a teen. Before he became a TV star? At Beverly Hills High, he played the Artful Dodger in a production of *Oliver!* —"

"Brianna, Dashiell was trying to point out the date," Shara said.

"Of the festival," Dashiell clarified. "At which Nolan will be. It's the same day as our play!"

Brianna stopped in her tracks. "Boo hiss. Why didn't we know this when we were setting dates?"

"Well, um, the stage manager usually does that," Dashiell said.

"Ouch." Brianna exhaled. "Okay, we need a Plan B. Who do we know who could kill him?"

"This is no laughing matter," said Dashiell, taking back the BlackBerry and shoving it in his pocket. "This could seriously impact our production."

"Can we change the date?"

"If we set it earlier, the play may not be ready," Dashiell said. "Any later, and we run into prep time for finals, not to mention an increased demand on the use of the cafeteria by other groups for end-of-the-year meetings and ceremonies and such. Mr. Levin has made it clear that Mr. Ippolito has made it clear that—"

"Okay, okay, let's not panic," Brianna said, stopping just outside the stairwell. "Maybe it's not so bad. Do you think we'll really lose people?"

"If they have a choice between seeing a play no one has ever heard of in a cafeteria, or meeting one of the hottest TV stars in the country in a beautiful waterfront setting with free food?" Shara asked.

"You're right," Brianna said. "We're screwed."

Downstairs, in Room 132, Casey sat nervously at the edge of a desk. She fingered a paper napkin with a pencil-drawn likeness of herself.

It was beautiful. Brett had done it, during lunch. And he was sitting in the middle of the room. Next to Chip.

They were both smiling at her.

Great. What was she supposed to do? Smile back, one at a time? Smile into the space between them?

She looked straight down. Pretended to be thinking about the upcoming scene. The fight, where Jack and his two friends jump Win. She was supposed to come in at the end of the scene and try to break it up. Then they were supposed to hurt her seriously. Knock her out. It would involve great physical coordination.

She had been dreading it all day.

Two new actors, Brian Johnson and Jeff Peterson, had been signed up to play Jack's friends. They waited politely in the front row, looking eager and excited.

Charles looked up from his script. "Okay, Win, Maya, Kayla, Jack, Carlos, and Mike!

"Top of scene. We are behind the line of buildings in a strip mall. Desolate. Dim lighting. The audience will be barely able to see what happens. Win enters one side of the stage, Jack and Kayla the other. Jack and Kayla expect a sale. Kayla has the stuff. Win says no. No money. No more drugs. Surprise, in walks Jack's two friends, Carlos and Mike. Fight, fight fight, blood and guts, Maya enters, gets caught up, et cetera. So, ready?"

Brian looked at Jeff. Jeff looked at Casey. Casey looked at Harrison.

"That's it?" Harrison said. "No stage direction?"

"Darlin', I'm a lover, not a fighter," Charles said. "Let's see what you boys come up with, shall we?"

"Are you trying to kill them?" shouted Reese, who was walking toward them from the back of the room. "Charles, you have to choreograph this! All fights are choreographed."

Charles gave her a look.

"You're not going to fire me, are you?" she asked, pinching Charles's butt.

"Ooh," said Charles. "Not if you do that."

"I'll start with the boys," Reese said, smiling seductively at Brian and Jeff, who looked like they'd just won the Lotto. "You and Casey go freshen up and come back in ten."

Charles held out his arm to Casey. "Follow the Yellow Brick Road?"

She smiled and took his arm. As they skipped out into the hallway, Charles surveyed some freshly painted flats that had been stacked against the wall. "Nice work," he said. "Now, are you going to tell me what's wrong?"

Casey wasn't expecting that. "What do you mean?"

"Don't try to hose Father Charles, honey," Charles said. "Confess and be saved."

Casey turned away, but Charles reached out and took her hand.

She looked into his deep brown eyes and wanted to cry. Wanted to tell him everything. All her confusion about Chip and Brett, her fears about the play. But all that came out was, "I—I suck, Charles. I don't know what I'm doing. I'm uncoordinated. I feel like everyone's laughing at me. Like I started out okay, but I'm just getting worse."

"Is *that* all?" Charles smiled. "Hon, welcome to the club. If I had a dime for each cast member who's said the same thing, I could leave for Aruba tomorrow. Well, maybe Jones Beach. Look at it this way—it's your *job* to get it wrong. That's what rehearsals are all about. *Rehearse* is the Latin word for 'screw up.'"

"Is that true?" Casey asked.

"I don't know. But it should be. You get it wrong now so you'll be *fabulous* on opening night. The ones who start out perfect in rehearsals are always the ones who have the most trouble."

Suddenly Reese's voice filtered in from Room 132. "Now, and-a ONE-two-three-four—step, step, *leap*, step!"

"What the—?" Charles jogged to the room and peered in. His jaw dropped.

When Casey joined him, she saw why. On direction from Reese, Brian and Jeff were doing some moves that looked like a cross between martial arts and *Dance Dance Revolution*. Harrison stood in the corner, looking dazed.

"Just a moment!" Charles shouted. "Uh, pardon me, Agnes de Mille, have we lost our marbles?"

"I figured it out, Charles!" Reese said excitedly, finger poised over a boom box. "I know what the play is missing. Not just a choreographed fight—but real *dance* choreography. Just watch. One-two-three-four!"

A hip-hop track blared out. Brian and Jeff looked at each other self-consciously.

"And—go!" Reese cried out.

The two boys started to move in sync. Shara burst out in a fit of giggles, Royce gave a hoot of laughter, and even Harrison struggled to keep a straight face.

Charles was too appalled to laugh. "Reese, darlin'," he said, "hilarity is not the emotional note we're going for in this scene. Show them how to fight without killing themselves. But lose the dance."

24

Monday, May 5, 3:57 P.M.

sprenglish: *yo. bad news. I have to cut the dc article. no room.*

Masterman0326: ru crazy, Artie? u guys always have too much room.

sprenglish: *not this time. we have an article about nolan now, prob 1000 wds or so.*

Masterman0326: who cares about that lowlife? hes gonna take people away from the show.

sprenglish: *snot our yob to help the dc, just to REPORT. And we've got a bunch of good pieces coming in.*

Masterman0326: this is good, artie. i promise.

sprenglish: *woodward and bernstein good?*

Masterman0326: is that all you think about?

sprenglish: *is there anything else?*

sprenglish: *look, unless u have something VERY juicy, very NOT boring, i don't want to hear about it. the world already knows a lot about the dc.*

Masterman0326: not the way i see them.

sprenglish: *yeah?*

Masterman0326: dude. i havent told u half of it. ive been working hard to get close.

sprenglish: *how close?*

Masterman0326: i'll tell u in person. better that way.

sprenglish: *cool. now ur thinking like a journalist. come on over.*

Masterman0326: u da man, bro.

sprenglish: *flattery will get u everywhere.*

"It's really great, Brett," said Casey into the phone. "I mean, I know you didn't want to do this—spoil your article by writing about the DC in your blog. But we can sure use the PR."

Brett laughed. He had a beautiful laugh. "Is that what you called to tell me?"

"Well, yeah . . ." Wasn't that a good enough reason? She had thought about it a lot. Not calling him would have been rude. That was all. "Did you think there was . . ."

"No!" Brett said. "I'm just surprised, that's all. Happy. People don't usually call just to say something nice. So thanks."

"Well, Shawn Nolan is going to be tough competition," Casey said.

"He doesn't have to be. There's lots you can do."

"What? Cry?"

"Hey, when the going gets tough," Brett said, "the tough get marketing." Casey heard the clattering of a keyboard. "I have an idea. What are you doing now?"

"Um . . ."

"I'm coming over in ten."

"Ten *minutes*—?"

Click.

Casey quickly looked at herself in the mirror. She was still a mess from rehearsing the fight scene that day. Her hair was sticking out at weird angles, and her shirt was all scuffed up. She looked terrible. No way could she greet Brett like this.

"Mom!" she called out, pulling her shirt over her head. "Please answer the doorbell when it rings. I'll be in the shower!"

* * *   IT'S NOT TOO LATE!!!   * * *

SEE THE PLAY **EVERYONE** IS TALKING ABOUT

EARLY ACTION

BY RIDGEPORT'S FUTURE

TONY®-AWARD-WINNING PLAYWRIGHT

CHIP DUGGAN

Thursday, May 29
8:00 P.M. !!

SAY YOU WERE AT THE HARBOR FESTIVAL

*AND GET IN FOR **FREE!!!***

"Poster number thirty-eight," Brett said, carefully taping a sign to a telephone pole on Duke Ellington Boulevard. "Two more."

"Wait," Casey said. "It's upside down."

"Oops," Brett said. He reached for it then pulled his hand back. "Actually, I kind of like it. It may attract more attention that way."

They were each down to their last poster. As Brett scurried across Ellington, Casey taped up hers. She looked down the street at their handiwork—each pole neatly decorated.

"Beautiful," Brett said.

"Are you sure this isn't, like, illegal?" Casey asked.

"Throwing us in jail would be the best publicity ever," Brett said. "Hey, we need eyes. And this is where they'll be."

"But it's deceptive. Everyone gets in for free even if they *don't* come to the festival. We're not charging admission."

Brett smiled slyly. "That's what you call salesmanship."

He opened his car's passenger door for Casey, and she climbed in. He ran around and got in the driver's side. As he turned the ignition, he gazed out the window. "Hmm. About fifteen minutes," he said.

"Do you really like doing that?" Casey asked.

"Doing what?" Brett replied.

"Saying things that don't make sense?"

"What didn't make sense?"

"'Fifteen minutes.'"

Brett leaned forward and peered out the windshield

again. "You're right. It's more like thirteen. We'd better go."

He pulled away from the curb and did a U-turn.

"Where?" Casey demanded.

"To the beach," Brett replied. "To see the sun set in thirteen minutes."

"But it's Sunday, and I've got a test—" Casey held tight. Brett was driving fast. She hated fast driving. By the time they reached the edge of town, she had unlocked her fingers from the armrest. When they finally swung onto the parkway, she settled back and watched the scenery go by. Gentle hills gave way to scrubby woods and fields where deer were coming out to graze.

By the time they arrived at Field 4 at Jones Beach, dusk was falling. The streetlamps already cast pools of light on the blacktop as they left the car and walked through the parking lot. At this time of the year there was only a small crowd. Brett offered his hand and she took it. They walked toward the beach through a landscaped walkway that was just beginning to show blossoms. She remembered this place . . . She was holding another hand then, her dad's, back before he left the family. "I haven't been here since I was little," Casey said. "It looks so much smaller than what I remember."

"You weren't here when Brianna nearly drowned?" Brett asked.

Casey looked over at him. "You heard about that?"

"I've heard all kinds of things since hanging with the DC. No details, though. Just general stuff."

As they emerged onto the boardwalk, Casey filled him

in on the details: Brianna's New Year's midnight swim with Kyle, her sneaking to steal her parents' drugs, all the pressure she had put on herself.

People were scattered along the length of the wooden walkway, alone or in small clusters, every group staying a polite distance from the other, all faces turned west.

The sun was enormous and swollen, its bottom just touching the surface of the ocean. "It happened over there," Casey said softly. "By the West End. Charles was the one who saved her life . . ."

"Charles is seriously underrated," Brett replied.

"I know." Casey nodded as their words dissipated into silence. Silence felt good with Brett. He was the kind of guy with whom it was okay to say nothing.

Gusts played against her face from all directions, sometimes warm, sometimes cool. She caught a heavy whiff of sea brine from the ocean, the sweet tang of lilac from the path. She closed her eyes and felt, for the first time in a long time, almost perfect.

The moment there was a hint of a chill, Brett's arm reached around her. She clasped her fingers gently around his forearm and held it close, smelling the faint sweetness of a freshly laundered shirt mixed with something else, something musty and boylike. He began to move, like a dance, slow and assured, his chest shifting across her back.

Oh God, what is happening what is happening WHAT IS HAPPENING?

Things would work out. That was what Brianna had said.

She had said it like an ancient truth. Like she'd experienced it firsthand so many times that it was like saying the sky was blue.

But the sky was never blue, and perfect was never perfect, and at that very moment Chip was somewhere not far away thinking all was okay between him and Casey, maybe smiling and calling her or sending an Instant Message or picking out a flavor of Ben & Jerry's ice cream for them to share.

And yet. And yet. Here at the beach Brett was leaning over her—so tall, all he had to do was bend over her right shoulder—and even with her eyes closed, she knew just where to turn, just how far to lean herself.

At this angle, looking up, her lips naturally fell open. She could have stopped them but there was no reason to, not when everything was so right, and the sun was chasing the year away, away into the deep, and Brett, who cared about her play and drew charcoal portraits on napkins, Brett, who talked nonsense and wrote poetry and was almost perfect, was kissing her.

26

"AM I HEARING AN ECHO?" CHARLES SAID TO REESE, walking toward the cafeteria. "Did we not have this discussion about dancing nasty boys? And didn't I veto it?"

"This is different," said Reese, trying to keep up with him. "I hadn't really thought it out before. What if it's a *dream sequence*? To *add* to the play. A new scene entirely. You see? Like in *Oklahoma!* and *Carousel*."

"Those are musicals," Charles said.

"Right. That's why this idea is so cool. It's like, where reality stops and fantasy begins. A rules change. Like, in the midst of the drama—surprise!—music. It's postmodern. Very *Moulin Rouge*. Okay, that's a movie. The boys have mastered the dance. It's all hip-hop, all street, totally appropriate—"

"Reese, doll," Charles said, turning to face her, "it is already May twelfth. We have dress rehearsal in ten days."

"And we have a new problem—competition from the festival!" Reese persisted. "We need something new and different—"

"Sweet buns, we are trying to *attract* people from Shawn Nolan, not chase them off. I tell you now what I told you the first time. No." Charles veered into the cafeteria, waving his finger in the air. "No. No. No!"

God, that felt good.

"Gooooood afternoon, campers," Charles said as he strode in. All around him, eager faces snapped to attention.

"Good afternoon, Charles!" they answered. Like Beaver Cleaver's classroom.

Charles liked being director. A lot. Actors listened better than Charlettes. If you crossed a Charlette, he could leave a thumbtack on the floor. Or a roller skate in your path. Or "forget" to set a telephone or a table or any number of absolutely necessary things, the absence of which made the actors look like fools.

That was the secret. Not making the actors look like fools. And who did they depend on to prevent that? The director!

So of course they listened.

Why had he not discovered this before?

He glanced at the set, which was taking shape nicely. The long cafeteria tables had been moved temporarily to make a staging area. To the left of it, Dashiell and his friend Ripley Grier were setting up a tree of theatrical lights, with the help of Shara. Vijay and the Rajputians were marking the floor with masking tape. Harrison, Casey, and the other cast members were running lines, spread around in different nooks and corners. Brett sat slumped in a chair, tapping away on his laptop.

Mr. Ippolito, the custodian, standing in the center of the cafeteria, nodded in greeting. "This is bringing it all back," he said. "We did a play here. Nineteen seventy-one. *You Can't Take It with You.* You'll never guess who I played. Go on, guess. Give up? Mr. DePinna!"

"No . . ." said Charles in mock disbelief.

"I knew that'd kill ya! Ha—that costume! Right?" Mr. Ippolito walked away, howling.

Reese raised an eyebrow. "Do you know the play?"

"Someone needs to brush up on her theater history," Charles told her. "It's a Kaufman and Hart comedy from the 1930s that just happened to win a Pulitzer." He glanced at the clock—3:45 on the dot. "Okay, let's begin where we left off—Act One, Scene Four! Win meets Maya. Win, you're on the hospital bed."

Vijay had wheeled in a bed and Harrison climbed on to it, absently holding a worn-out stuffed animal.

"Hi," said Casey, as Maya.

Harrison looked up. He hid the stuffed animal behind his back. Looked back. Didn't answer.

"Do you talk?" Casey asked tentatively.

Harrison looked away.

"What's your name?" Casey asked. Then she sat on the edge of the bed and laughed playfully. "Okay, what's the name of your stuffed pal?"

Harrison mumbled, "Biffalo Buff."

"From Dr. Seuss?" Casey said.

Harrison's eyes flickered then died out.

"From the *Sneetches* book. I know it." Casey leaned in and tickled him, and Harrison bolted to his feet.

Nice, Charles thought. The tension was crisp and uncomfortable.

"Okay, okay, I won't do it again . . . damn," Casey said. "If you ever want to talk, I'm on the floor below. You look familiar. Do I know you?"

Harrison turned away.

"Oh, well. Someone who likes Dr. Seuss can't be all bad," Casey said before exiting.

Charles watched intently. Harrison was good—but he was always good. The big news was Casey. She seemed so natural today. She looked like a real person, not an actor trying to remember blocking.

He glanced back at Chip, who was watching her intently.

Love was always a nice thing for one's self-esteem, Charles thought. Casey was lucky.

Casey could feel the note in her pocket, but she blocked it out. The rehearsal was working. She had never felt anything like it before. As if real life had faded to practically nothing, with just an occasional reminder— a note, a glint from the cafeteria lunch rack, a distant squeak from someone's iPod. But as soon as it came, it disappeared.

Through most of the rehearsal, Casey felt her pulse had slowed to nothing. Like she was in some dreamworld.

Like all her emotions—the anger, the confusion, the playfulness—were coming from somewhere else, flowing through her. Memorizing lines wasn't even a thought—they were there, in her mouth.

"And don't ever let me see you do that again!" Casey screamed, storming off the "stage."

End of scene.

That was it. Harrison looked after her. Silently. Glassy-eyed. As if he had a million things he wanted to say, but couldn't. He sat there like that, staring blankly, as the lights slowly dimmed.

The clapping started at the back of the cafeteria—Royce, probably. Then, one by one, the others joined in, until the place was echoing with whoops and applause.

"I'm having hot flashes, kids!" Charles said, shouting above the applause. "That was brilliant! *We have turned a corner!* What a note to end the rehearsal on!"

Casey wanted to let it soak in. It *had* gone well. But now the spell was broken. Everything real, the things of life that had been tucked away, were spilling out.

She could feel Chip's eyes on her. He was smiling. So happy and triumphant. He deserved to be. His hard work had paid off. His play was incredible now, start to finish.

He didn't know about her and Brett. He didn't suspect a thing.

But she had to tell him.

Casey grabbed her jacket. The tears that had been threatening to burst forth now began flowing down her cheek. She had to get out before anyone saw her. She waved good-bye and put her head down, then barreled through the lobby and out the door.

She couldn't face him. Couldn't bear to look into his eyes.

The note. He would be expecting her to respond to it.

He had grabbed her hand at the beginning of the rehearsal. Pressed the note into it. A haiku. It was still in her pocket. As she headed onto the sidewalk, she pulled it out and unfolded it:

> I lurked in shadows
> Never knowing who I was
> Until I met you.
>
> Thanks, Casey. We're getting there.
> I owe this to you. All of it.
> Chip

Casey brushed away tears, which were flowing freely now.

Now what? What could she say? What could she tell him? She'd never been in a situation like this. She was the girl everyone thought was so nice. So trustworthy. But that wasn't the reality. She was the betrayer.

It had felt so *right* at the beach last night. She hadn't hesitated for a moment when Brett leaned over to kiss her. Never a doubt. She probably could have pushed aside a nuclear attack at that moment. Nothing else seemed to matter.

BEEEP! BEEEEP!

Casey jumped. At the curb, Brett's car rumbled to a stop. The automatic window on the passenger side rolled down. Inside, Brett leaned across the bucket seats. "Hey, do you need a ride?"

"No, thanks!" Casey said, trying to muster as much cheerfulness as she could. "I'm fine."

She heard the ratchety sound of the handbrake, and saw Brett looking up at her. "Hey—you sure?"

He was reaching for her but she held back. Forced a smile. It was wrong now. It didn't feel at all like it did the day before. "Fine. It was a long rehearsal, Brett. I—I sort of need a little space, that's all."

He backed away, but she couldn't look at his face.

Hooking her bag tightly over her arm, she hurried away.

27

From: <scopascetic@rport.li.com>
To: CAST_AND _CHARACTERS
Sent: Sunday, May 25, 6:35 P.M.
Subject: DRESS!!!!!!!!!
Yes, boys and girls—it's time!!! Don't forget to bring your costumes on Wednesday (that's in THREE DAYS!!!!) to our one and only DRESS REHEARSAL!!! Harrison, do NOT throw away that ripped shirt, it's fab. Barry and Jen, NOTHING from H&M, please, if I have to go to Brooks Brothers myself to dress you, I will. Let me know. And Brianna, darling, thank you for dropping in, thank you for the emails, and I AM SO GLAD TECH WEEK STARTS TOMORROW, CUZ WE NEED YOU NOW!!
Toodles, CS

"It's fluorescent," Dashiell said, handing Brianna a thick roll of tape. "I chose it to match, more or less, the color of the linoleum tiles. So when stage lights are on, you won't see it, but when it's dark—bingo! I realized we needed this yesterday, when Dino knocked over the light tree, costing us twenty-eight dollars and thirty-seven cents in halogen-bulb replacement."

"Yes, sir," Brianna said.

"And take this," Dashiell added, handing her a headset.

"Thanks." She put on the headset, took the tape, and quickly began outlining the area around the base of the lighting tree with fluorescent tape.

Brianna breathed in deeply. Yup, she could smell it. The air was always different near performance time. Charged. Electric. She could hardly believe tech week was in full swing and it was already dress rehearsal! So much had happened before this week, during her self-imposed exile. Dashiell had managed to light the cafeteria with so much originality that it really did look like a stage. People were respecting Charles—even Harrison. And what she had seen of the play was pretty good. Chip was the real deal.

"CAN YOU HEAR ME?"

"Aaagh!" Brianna nearly fell over. "Where's the volume control, Dashiell?"

"LEFT EAR!"

She found the knob, turned it down, and continued marking the floor with tape. Then she began carefully lining the place where the floor met the wall. This way actors could follow the tape right to the exit.

Harrison was standing in her way, near the door, warming up his voice. "Mama's a mean mama, mama's a mean mama, mama's a mean mama, mama's a mean mama . . ." he sang on a descending scale.

"Excuse me," Brianna said.

"Baby's a bad baby, baby's a bad baby, baby's a bad baby, baby's a bad baby, baby's a bad baby . . ." Harrison sang.

Brianna taped his foot to the floor.

"Brianna banana, Brianna banana, Brianna banana, Brianna banana . . ."

As she began untying his shoelaces, he darted away, laughing, the ripped piece of fluorescent tape dangling from his shoe like broken wings.

There was so much to do. Dashiell's cues to be memorized and gone over. Entrances and exits to be reviewed. New cue lines to be written onto the cue sheets. Costume problems to be assigned to the Charlettes—er, Rajputians.

She went back to her seat and picked up her marked-up script.

Charles pulled up the seat next to her. "I am *so* glad you're here," he said.

"How are advance tickets going?" Brianna asked.

"How should I know?" Charles said. "We are free admission. A people's production. No reserved seats, come if you feel like it. We don't even know how many seats to set up."

Brianna eyed Casey, who was pacing along the side of the cafeteria. "What's up with Case?"

Charles smiled. "Oh Lord, honey, you *have* been away."

Someone slipped a touch of Meryl Streep powder into her Vitamin Water this week. She's *preparing.*"

Brett, looking like he hadn't washed his tousled hair in a day or two, rushed into the cafeteria with his laptop. "Hey, Charles. How much longer till you start?"

Charles looked at his watch. "One minute ago."

"I don't want to miss this experience," Brett said, settling into a seat. "A real DC dress rehearsal. *Has* to be part of my article. Artie's gonna have to wait."

"You haven't written the article yet?" Brianna asked. "But the show is—"

"Tomorrow, I know," Brett said. "Artie got the printer to agree to a rush job. They'll have the paper ready on the night of the first performance."

Charles's face fell. "The article has to happen *before* the show. To give us some publicity. It doesn't help us if it comes out *afterward.*"

Brett shrugged. "At least it'll be out before the second show."

Charles paled, but said, "Yet one more challenge, duckies. I suppose we'll just have to triumph anyway."

Dashiell's voice blared out over the speakers: "*Brianna, do you read me!*"

Brianna hopped away. The next ten minutes went by in a blur of troubleshooting, complaints, and rapid-fire learning, until finally Charles called for places.

"Places!" Brianna repeated, scanning her clipboard. "Mom, Dad, Win—onstage, please! *Places!*"

The clamor in the cafeteria died down. As Jenny and Barry took their places on the right side of the stage and Harrison on the left, the cafeteria went black.

Slowly a warm amber light illuminated the right side of the stage, which had been somehow transformed into a dream of the perfect American living room. Jenny and Barry bustled in, dressed in corporate outfits. Jenny, holding an armful of mail, spilled almost all of it in her excitement to get to the armchair.

On stage left, a mirror ball descended from the ceiling, scattering fractured light across the cafeteria. Throbbing music began to pulse, the bass cranked way up. Harrison, transformed somehow into a thin, geeky nerd, stood looking scared and overwhelmed. In his right hand he held a drink.

"Music up, stage left," Brianna whispered into the headset mike. "Lights up, stage right."

As Harrison sipped, he began to dance.

And Barry's hand slowly reached for the thick envelope.

Part 3
Unplugged

May 29

28

"GOD BLESS AMERICA AND DON'T FORGET THE Greeks!"

Harrison cringed. His father was here. On opening night.

How many years had he resented his dad's *absences* at DC productions? For most of Harrison's high school career, his father would cater rehearsals and make friends with the actors, but never actually *come to* a show—"because I am *working* at night!" Then, finally, he managed to see *Grease*. And now they couldn't keep him away.

Which should be a good thing, except for the fact that wherever Kostas Michaels went, he *was* the show.

In the corner, Casey was deep in conversation with

Brianna. Chip and Charles were discussing a tweak to Act One. Reese was doing high kicks, and Jenny was adjusting Barry's wig.

Harrison turned away from the voice. From the sound of the preshow hysterics. The distractions. In the new environment, so many adjustments had to be made. Like using the hallway behind the cafeteria as an impromptu Green Room. Because everyone else was running around, it forced you to concentrate. To survive, to keep focus, you had to block out the noise.

"DUDE!"

A pair of arms reached around him from behind and lifted him off the ground. "Break a leg and an arm!" It was Kyle, without a crutch, his ankle wrapped in a Frankenstein-style surgical boot.

"Hey, you guys, say cheese!" Brett called out.

Kyle released Harrison, and they both turned to see Brett pointing a camera at them.

"Cheese this!" said Kyle, turning quickly and mooning him just as the flash went off.

"Auughhhh, you broke my lens," Brett said.

Kyle pumped his fist. "Yyyyyess! Classic!"

"Go away," Harrison replied, flipping Brett the middle finger.

Click.

"Break a leg!" Brett said, ducking back into the cafeteria.

"Been there, done that," said Kyle, limping away.

Harrison closed his eyes.

Focus.

In his mind, he was no longer Harrison. He was Win, perfect student. Perfect everything. Walking through life on a tightrope of perfect. He heard Brianna call out, *"Five minutes!"* and then, *"Places!"* He heard squeals and screams and well wishes. And then Charles's announcement:

"Ladies and gentlemen, thank you all for coming. This is a unique performance in the history of the Drama Club—our first-ever original play!"

Harrison stood by the door. He breathed deeply, not really hearing the rest of the speech. Letting the transformation be complete. And when Brianna finally whispered, "Go," into his ear, he was ready.

Pathetic, Brianna thought.

She stood in the darkness at the back of the cafeteria, watching as Vijay escorted two latecomers to their seats, about five minutes into the first act.

That made fifteen people. *Fifteen.*

Which doubly, triply, a thousand times sucked, because the play was so good. Harrison especially, bless his heart, was amazing.

If only they hadn't set up so many seats. Close to a hundred, probably. Plus they had kept another hundred chairs folded up nearby, just in case. Bad, bad decision. Now, with the tiny cluster of people gathered in the middle, the empty chairs made the whole production seem lame.

She had *never* seen a turnout like this. Ridgeport was all about sellout crowds, SRO audiences. Poor Chip. He must be devastated.

Brianna looked around. Where *was* Chip? Maybe in the hallway, crying. Or beating a fast retreat home, to suffer in silence.

In her mind, she was burning Shawn Nolan at the stake. His deep dimples were filling with smoke and his cute curly hair was whipping upward in flames. *That* was where most Ridgeporters were tonight, getting his autograph and eating greasy food by the waterfront.

It wasn't fair.

She glanced at Dashiell. He stood several feet to her side, operating the light board. The cues had gone off almost perfectly, just a couple of minor glitches. Like the actors, Dashiell was all about concentration and focus. She needed to be that way, too.

Onstage, Mom and Dad had just dropped Win off at the Gowanus Hospital. Harrison—as Win—was holding a cup with his meds, looking lost. Around him, the cast was boisterous, screaming. Shara, playing Kayla, the drug-dealing sociopath, threw a tantrum on the phone, flinging the receiver across the room. "Lockdown! Lockdown!" came a voice over the speakers, and the kids who played orderlies swept in and began herding the patients into another room.

Slowly the voices faded, so that everyone was in pantomime, laughter and resistance and screaming totally silent. As the stage lights went down, a pin spotlight, white-hot, went up on Harrison in the midst of it all as he turned slowly toward the audience, looking scared out of his mind.

Then, blackout.

The audience sat in stunned silence. And they stayed that way, through the entire first act—Win's first meeting with Maya, his first purchase of drugs from Jack, and his violent reaction in the hospital cafeteria.

Brianna didn't have a chance to hang around and listen to audience comments during intermission. She was too busy helping Dashiell fix a broken light board. The beginning of the second act passed in a blur—Win's solitary confinement, his release from the hospital, his reuniting with his parents, and a comic scene at a golf club where a group of Type-A incoming Harvard freshmen nearly gore him in a game of killer volleyball.

She made sure to watch the scene where Kayla sells Win painkillers after his release. Harrison always nailed that—the hope of recovery smashed by a drug deal. And then, slowly, the descent.

As the lights went up on Scene Five, Barry paced the living-room set. "This has been hard for all of us, Win," he said. "But we have to pick ourselves up and move forward. Otherwise life passes us by. You have a golden opportunity, and from what I'm seeing, you're just retreating into bad habits and bad associations."

Harrison turned slowly. His eyes seemed bloodshot. He looked, somehow, as if he had lost ten pounds during the play. Suddenly he shot up out of his chair. When he spoke, his voice was like a grenade. *"Is my life any of your fucking business?"*

Oops.

Instantly Brianna heard Dashiell's whispered voice in her headphone: "Did he just say the F-word?"

Brianna exhaled. "Mm-hm," she murmured.

"He did, he said the F-word," Dashiell murmured in disbelief.

She looked for Mr. Levin in the audience, but the "house" was dark, and she couldn't see him.

A few feet from her, Charles was rubbing his forehead. He gave Brianna a what-are-ya-gonna-do kind of a shrug.

Brianna grinned. Harrison was just doing his job— being real. Pulling back on obscenities, substituting blander words, made no sense. It sounded phony.

From that point on, Harrison was on fire. His nerdiness curdled into nastiness. His face began to look feral, sneering. He was totally convincing as a drug addict. His attack on Casey made Charles jump in his seat and drew a gasp from someone in the audience.

The aftermath, with Harrison holding Casey, crying, confessing his drug habit, had not worked that well in rehearsal—but it was perfect tonight. His speech about opening up, about allowing himself to be himself, made Brianna cry. That was a good sign.

She braced herself for the end. In the second-to-last scene, Harrison had drenched himself. He looked sweaty, drug-sweaty, running across the stage, looking over his shoulder. *"Jack!"* he cried out. *"Kayla! You bastards, where are you?"*

"Dude," said Hassan, who was playing Jack. He came out of the shadows with a big smile. "Sounds like you need my help."

Harrison seemed to be looking at him from some distant planet. "No," he said. "I'm here to tell you something."

"Anything, my friend," Hassan said.

"If you ever bother me again, I will turn you in."

Hassan smiled easily. "You didn't say that."

"Look, I want out. That's all. It's over, Jack."

Hassan snapped his fingers.

From each side of the stage, out of Harrison's line of sight, came a figure in silhouette—Jeff with a pipe, Brian with a knife.

"I'm sure I can convince you to reconsider, Winthrop."

Harrison shook his head. "Not a chance, dude." He turned and began to walk away purposefully.

Hassan turned to the other two with a grim, barely perceivable nod.

Brianna didn't like watching this. She turned her back and listened to the scrapes and scuffles, Casey's entrance . . . utter chaos.

And then, above it all, Harrison's primal, animal scream.

She hated this part. He had rehearsed it only once before. It was an inhuman scream that seemed to well up from his toes, a sound so loud that it blocked all thought, made Brianna's own voice ache for the pain it must be causing Harrison's.

It echoed in the cafeteria, turning over twice before decaying into silence.

And there they were, center stage, in the spot, Casey in Harrison's arms. "Maya," Harrison said, over and over, his voice sandpapery hoarse.

As the police-light effect hit the stage, bathing them

in whiteness, Casey's eyes opened. She smiled weakly at Harrison.

Blackout.

In the ensuing silence, Brianna realized that Charles had sidled up to her. He rested his cheek on her shoulder, and she thought she felt the warm moisture of tears. Dashiell, his face dimly lit by the glow of the light board, let the darkness last a few dramatic seconds. Then, slowly, he raised the cafeteria lights, signaling that the play was officially over.

Silently, the cast left the cafeteria stage, exiting into the hallway. Brianna's heart was pounding. Charles lifted his head. He looked at her with alarm.

There was no sound. Nothing.

The audience was sitting there, inert.

We bombed, Brianna said to herself. The play hadn't worked. They'd been deluding themselves. *No one liked it.*

She slumped into a chair next to Charles.

And then, from the front row, came one strong, steady hand clap. *"Etsi, bravo!"*

Mr. Michaels.

The hallway door opened. As the cast came in for curtain calls, the audience finally came to life. Sort of. A whistle sounded in the back. A loud *"Yeah!"*

Kyle.

The rest of them were sitting, clapping politely as the actors with the smaller roles took their bows. Mr. Michaels stood, and so did Kyle. A couple of other audience members joined them.

By the time the principal actors came out for their

bows, the applause was louder and warmer. Charles stepped to the front and thanked everyone. He gestured to Mr. Levin, who took a small bow. The audience filed out, murmuring among themselves, some of them nodding toward Brianna and Dashiell.

And that was it. Fifteen people could clear a cafeteria pretty fast.

Brianna watched the door shut. She heard hubbub in the hallways, where some of the audience were talking to the cast.

Now the room was empty except for Charles, Reese, Brianna, Mr. Levin, and Kyle, who had stuck around.

"What happened?" Dashiell said, shaking his head in disbelief.

"They hated us," Charles replied. "But I don't get it. I thought everyone did so well."

"Kids," Mr. Levin said, strolling over from his seat in the corner. "Two things. One, even with such a small audience, I have a feeling that we're going to be hearing about Harrison's one-word improv. Two, I'm willing to take the heat, because it worked. I don't care if only one person came to this play. I don't care if no one comes to the next show. This was one of the finest nights in the theater I've ever had."

"Totally awesome!" said Kyle.

Putting on her best possible face, Brianna began to strike the stage.

They were going to have to go back out and do it again on Saturday.

29

The Ridgeport Rambler

Drama Club Unplugged

by Brett Masters

How many actors does it take to change a lightbulb?

Five hundred! One to change the bulb and 499 to say, "I could have done that part!"

It's an old joke, known to every actor on Broadway. For two years I've been like those 499 actors—trying, trying, trying to make it into a Drama Club production only to realize that hey, face it, I suck.

Sound familiar? You too, right?

Well, at least that's what the Drama Club would have you think. *They* are the actors, the future stars.

As for us—the peons—we are lucky to have them, and if we know what's good for us, we'll be their friends. Because someday they just *might* get us free tickets to their Broadway shows.

Yup, face it, that's been the perceived wisdom here at Ridgeport for decades. But is it true? That's what I wanted to find out.

So . . . shazzzzzzzzam! Enter Masterman, to break through the fourth wall and find out the truth behind RHS theater.

Ever wonder what really goes on in those backstage rooms? Or what happens *after* the posters are put up to publicize the show? Or why the same people seem to be cast for the same roles? Or why those guys always seem to have big smiles on their faces?

As Masterman has discovered, in the DC, the Real Drama is behind the stage, not in front . . .

"Tell me this is some kind of a joke." Charles stared at the article in astonishment.

"He hosed us," Harrison snapped, seething, throwing the newspaper back on the top of the pile, which stood in front of the school newspaper office. "He totally hosed us—*and we helped him do it!*"

The smell of the newsprint filled the hallway. Casey could see the Ridgeport Printing Press truck pulling away from the curb outside. It had just dropped off the papers—on opening night, as promised. Harrison, in his excitement, had cut the plastic binding and taken the top copy.

It had been hard enough playing to a mostly empty house. But to find this on the way out? It was the kick in the teeth after the gut punch.

"Casey, do you know anything about this?" Harrison asked.

Casey shook her head. Her eyes scanned the article. It got worse as it went on. The story of Gabe and Deena. A reference to Harrison and Brianna hooking up—and another to Harrison and Reese. A description of the snarky remarks the DC officers made about auditioners—including Sandra McGill's "Martian accent." Lots of detail about the fight between Charles and Harrison. And a line about Mr. Levin, being more of a friend than a faculty adviser, turning a conveniently blind eye, not daring to interfere with the "real business" of the DC.

And then there it was:

Membership does have its rewards. Unlike normal people, there are no barriers, no awkward moments. All arms are open in the DC. The "good cheer" is found everywhere: high notes reached (and windows steamed) in the instrument rehearsal rooms, for *Godspell*. A wintry skinny-dip with Jesus and his luckiest disciple. Some creative dance moves between one leading man and his acrobatic dance partner, during *Grease*. LUV is in the air, and you fall all over it, wherever you go—for the lucky ones. Even this writer couldn't help but be drawn into the fun, on a sunset night at Jones Beach with a willing and able DC cast member who shall remain nameless. Hey, kids, hop aboard—in the Drama Club, when you're in, you're in . . .

Casey's breathing shortened. As if someone had taken the air out of the room.

Drawn into the fun?

Is that what it was?

Willing and able?

Who shall remain nameless?

Casey's eyes blurred. How could Brett do this? How could a human being do something like this?

This was not the guy who had taken her to the beach. Who had been so gentle and warm.

She had trusted him. Confided in him. Told him everything. About Brianna's breakdown. About herself.

He had turned her life inside out, made her doubt Chip—loyal, trustworthy, *real* Chip—and for what? For *this*? Was *this* why he'd taken her to the beach? For material? Had he run home afterward and written everything down? Had he recorded their conversation?

"It—it can't be," Casey murmured.

"He said he was our friend," Charles said.

"We trusted him," Harrison added.

"Let's burn the newspapers," Reese suggested.

"No," Brianna said. "I want to talk to him. I want an explanation. I want him *on his knees*. And then I'll kill the creep."

"It's not even well written," Charles said under his breath.

"He left early, the son of a bitch," Harrison said. "I'm going over to his house now."

"No," Casey blurted out. She might be uncertain about a lot of things in life—but on this she could not have been surer. *She* needed to be the one to hear Brett's explanation. "Let me go."

She folded up one of the newspapers and put it into her pocket. Without saying another word, she left.

The walk to Brett's house was long, but Casey didn't care. She barely noticed the blossoms, the fragrance of spring. It was all she could do to keep from screaming.

The red car was parked in the driveway. An Arctic Monkeys song was blaring out of a dormer window, his bedroom. She stormed up the front stairs and rang the doorbell.

She could hear his voice now, whiny and out of tune, trying to sing along.

He *did* suck. His voice was atrocious. How *dare* he suggest that the auditions had somehow been rigged against him? She banged on the door, and when he didn't answer she banged again, punching it as hard as she could.

Suddenly the music stopped. She heard the thumping of footsteps on the stairs, and then the front door opened.

Brett grinned when he saw her face. "Heyyyy, Casey!"

He was *grinning*.

The alpha dog.

The winner.

The son of a bitch.

"You—" Casey's brain was firing in a hundred different

directions—anger, humiliation, betrayal, and the wish to commit murder all vying for dominance. "You ASSHOLE!"

His smile vanished. "Casey?"

She pulled the newspaper from her pocket, ripped it in half, and threw it on his living-room floor.

She turned and walked away before she left her heart there, too.

30

May 30, 11:47 P.M.

dramakween: ru ok, casey?

changchangchang: yeah. thanks, bri

dramakween: hes the worst

changchangchang: yeah. i cant believe how stupid
i was.

dramakween: we all were

dramakween: did you talk to him?

changchangchang: i could barely say a word, bri.
i was so mad. all i wanted to do was cry, but i didn't
want him to see that.

changchangchang: so i kinda melted down in front
of him. ripped up the newspaper etc.

dramakween: my hero. ☺

changchangchang: that's what ive been doing all night.

dramakween: *ripping newspapers?*

changchangchang: crying. i cant stop. i feel so betrayed.

dramakween: *i am devising all kinds of ways to get back at him.*

changchangchang: don't. don't even think about him anymore. as far as I'm concerned, he doesn't exist. i'm just worried about chip. he left in the middle of the show & i cant reach him. cell, im, etc. he doesn't respond.

dramakween: *do u think he knows about the article?*

changchangchang: god i hope not.

dramakween: *i don't think people will take it seriously. let's just make the last show great. hey, the worst is over, right?*

changchangchang: right!

May 31, 6:27 P.M.

Harrison glanced away from the clock in the Ridgeport High A/V room and back to the old twenty-six-inch TV set. A Toyota commercial was showing a breathless drive up some impossible alpine slope that only an idiot would ever attempt by car.

Brianna, Reese, Casey, and Dashiell all sat forward in various chairs, munching on popcorn. There was only an hour before "half hour," when they would have to get ready for the second show, but they had all arrived early. Deciding to go through with the second show had been hard. After opening night's poor turnout and Brett's article in the *Rambler*, Brianna had suggested canceling. Practically no one in school had mentioned the play on Friday, just a couple of die-hard DC fans who had been in the audience. In fact, it had been about the most depressing Friday Harrison could remember. But Mr. Levin encouraged them to go ahead, reminding them that the Harbor Festival was over and Shawn Nolan was "back in his glamorous villa eating bonbons and sunning by the pool."

Then came the rumors.

They had been flying around the school and all over town yesterday and today. Charles had heard at the bookstore that *Early Action* had nudity and simulated sex. Reese had been scolded outside the hardware store by the owner, old Mr. Sedgewick, who said the theater had never been the same after the hippies wrecked it. Brianna found a blog on a conservative Web site that said Ridgeport's "education charter" should be revoked for the foul language allowed onstage.

Brianna's dad was the one who had found out about the *Six O'Clock News* coverage. Now, as the commercial ended, the local TV newscaster Jake Jarvis appeared with his close-cropped black hair.

He was looking somber today. "Well, as Shakespeare might say, there's something rotten in the village of Ridgeport—as a controversy brews about a famous group of high-school thespians . . ."

Charles groaned. "I hate when they use that word. Can't they say *actors*?"

"Ssshhhh," said Harrison.

The scene faded to the counter of Chandra's Superette in downtown Ridgeport, where Chandra, the shop owner, was smiling nervously at the camera. "Well, you know kids," she said, "they get a little publicity, and they think they can do anything . . ."

"Augggh, and I'm always so nice to her," Brianna said.

A priest from a church in a nearby town solemnly intoned, "I'm as tolerant of free speech as the next person, but foul language has no place in a public high school."

"I am not paying taxes to fund this kind of crap," said someone identified as a Ridgeport resident. "'Cause that's what it is. There's no redeeming value, you know what I mean?"

Then came Jarvis's voice, over a montage of photos, beginning with the ones used in the *New York Times* article a few years back: "The *Times* called them 'a hothouse for Broadway talent,' with tales of parents who move to Ridgeport with their theatrically talented kids to give them a leg up on a performing career. But in recent years, as learned by WWLI, the publicity just may have gone to their heads . . ."

The images suddenly changed:

Kyle mooning the camera, the crucial parts pixilated . . . Harrison flipping the bird, his face (and finger) also blotted out—*Brett's photos*! Harrison as Win in *Early Action*, popping pills . . . attacking Casey, ripping her shirt . . .

"I don't believe this," Brianna groaned as Jarvis's voice-over continued:

". . . culminating in Friday night's performance of an

original drama written by a Ridgeport High junior in which portrayals of drug addiction, rape, suicide attempts, and uncensored language allegedly ran rampant . . ."

"They used . . . oh, goodness, can I say it? . . . the F-word," said an old man, his face fading in over the montage. "If I did that at their age, I was grounded for a week."

Then an image of the *Ridgeport Rambler* masthead appeared as Jarvis's voice continued: ". . . and an exposé in the student-run newspaper portrayed a club of insiders, monopolizing roles, using school property for possibly illegal activity—not to mention a total lack of supervision by the authorities . . ."

Jarvis himself reappeared on the screen, shaking his head. "Gee, Miranda, you hate to hear things like this, don't you?"

The camera panned back to reveal a blond woman with tons of makeup. "Indeed, Jake. Let's take a look at tomorrow's weather . . ."

Harrison flipped off the TV. "Illegal activity? *Illegal activity?*" he said.

Reese sighed. "I think they airbrushed what was left of Kyle's butt."

"You would know," Charles remarked.

She elbowed him sharply.

"Where did they *get* those photos?" Dashiell asked.

"Blogs, Facebook, whatever," Brianna said.

"Brett took them," Harrison said. "Or the worst of them."

"The traitor," Charles grumbled.

"I tried to IM him," Harrison said. "He was off-line."

Casey stood up. "I think we should just ignore all this. Brett can't destroy us. Nobody can. And we didn't do anything wrong."

"Damn straight," Charles said. "I mean, *damned* straight."

"Has anyone seen Chip?" Dashiell asked. "He is the one most likely to take this the hardest."

Casey shook her head. "He disappeared right after the show began on Thursday. I keep calling his house, and his mom keeps telling me he's at the library."

With a resounding *thwack*, the door flew open and smacked against the wall. Mr. Levin, looking slightly dazed, poked his head in. "*There* you are! I've got to show you something."

He darted out the door. Harrison leaped up and ran after him. The others followed close behind, through the hallways and into one of the classrooms on their floor, the second. The windows overlooked the front of the school. "Take a look," Mr. Levin said.

A line stretched from the front door all the way down the sloping lawn to the street, then snaked at least half a block southward.

Harrison couldn't believe his eyes. "What the—?"

"Is that for *us*?" Brianna said.

"Oh, yes it is," Charles said. "Looks like our loyal fans haven't deserted us after all."

"I'm not sure it's that simple," said Mr. Levin, his tone wary. "But we'll talk later. Let's just get on with the show."

They started toward the cafeteria, with Mr. Levin at the end of the procession. Harrison held back a little, drawing even with the teacher. "You're not thrilled about this crowd," he said uneasily. "Do you think there's going to be trouble?"

Mr. Levin hesitated a moment before replying. "Don't you guys get it? There already is."

31

IT HAPPENED SO FAST.

By the end of the play, Casey could barely remember what had happened at the beginning.

It all came back to her after the curtain call, in a flash of mental images:

The chairs. So many to set up. Even the audience had jumped in. It was a strange feeling, a roll-up-your-sleeves kind of excitement. It joined cast, crew, and audience into one big family.

The mass. As the lights went down, Casey saw them—the audience—for the first time, really saw them through the door. It was as if they had replaced the air in the room. They sat wall to wall. Latecomers, who'd had to park a block away, were climbing over knees with muttered

"Excuse me"s and "Nice to see you"s. Like the big Spring Musical, only more so. As if Thursday had been a kind of warp-drive trip into a parallel reality, where Ridgeport had, for one day only, ceased being a theater town.

The intro. "Wow . . . WOW!" was the way Charles had begun it, throwing away his scripted speech and making the crowd applaud for themselves.

The gravity. Or lack thereof. Like the laws of physics had gone totally whack. In the hallway Casey felt weightless, as if she were floating from hug to hug on a sea of squeals and laughter. As if the crowd itself had snatched up all the gravity into a big dense black hole. You could feel it when you went onstage.

The calm. Onstage she didn't have the luxury of being nervous. Not with so many eyes focused on her. Brianna had told her that the bigger the crowd, the calmer the nerves. But Casey hadn't believed it until tonight.

The flow. Barry, in his scenes, had seemed to grow thirty years and thirty pounds. His wig somehow had settled into a less helmetlike, more *real* shape. Even his voice sounded old. Jenny, supposedly the weakest link, was nailing every line. Casey's scenes with Harrison were tense and fast. No unexpected rips or stumbles, no dropped lines or missed cues. After the big attack, there was an audible gasp from the audience.

The end. This was the biggest shock.

After all that, after all the differences between the two performances, the reaction was *totally the same.*

No one applauded.

The lights went out to sheer silence. It was exactly like

opening night. In the darkness of the hallway, Casey had grabbed Brianna's hand and squeezed hard. She couldn't even bring herself to ask where they had gone wrong.

"What happened?" whispered Royce.

When the response began, it was like a beast awakening from hibernation. Not a gradual swell, but a shock of cheering. It grew large, filling the cafeteria, filling the hallway with the pounding of hands, the shouts and cheers and whistles. For a long moment the cast stood frozen, no one paying attention to Brianna's shouts into the hallway for "curtain call!"

"Go! Go! Go!" Charles shouted, waving his arms like a windmill.

The ensemble characters raced out first, and the cheering grew even louder. Barry and Jenny got a huge response.

Casey waited her turn. She was supposed to go with Harrison, but he pushed her on by herself, and she stood at the center, bowing and crying, letting the character of Maya out of her head and this—this noise—in.

Casey's mom was in the third row, cheering, weeping, throwing her kisses. Casey had been afraid her mother might freak out in a bad way, but this was a good reaction, better than she could have imagined. She could feel the tears flowing, blocking her vision, and although she completely forgot to signal for Harrison, he ran out on his own, taking her hand and planting a gentle kiss on her cheek as they both bowed . . . and then bowed again, with the whole cast, letting the sound embrace them. It felt as if the crowd would never stop, never let them go.

"We did it! We were brilliant!" Charles screamed as they all finally retreated back into the hallway.

Casey hugged Charles. "You were the best director!"

"Who'da thunk it, huh?" he said, swinging her around like a rag doll. "And *you*, my dear—you were sensational!"

"He's here!" Harrison cried out, pulling Casey by her shirt. "Chip is here—I saw him."

Casey followed him back into the cafeteria, where two gray-haired couples had cornered Chip. "Oh," he said, glancing at Casey. "Uh, these are my parents and my aunt and uncle. I was just explaining the unfolding of the dramatic structure as a kind of sonata form—theme, development, and recapitulation—excuse me . . ."

He took Casey by the hand and led her down the hallway and around the corner.

When he spun around to face her, his eyes were solemn. She swallowed hard. Part of her wanted to wrap him up in a big hug. But the adrenaline was flowing away fast. "It went well tonight," he said.

Casey smiled. "We—I—missed you."

"Did you?" Chip asked.

"Are you kidding? Chip, I've been worried sick. You kind of disappeared. None of us could get hold of you."

"I was feeling nervous," Chip said. "I couldn't . . ."

His voice trailed off and he didn't say anything for a long time. When he finally looked at her, his eyes were unreadable. "The 'willing and able' DC cast member— that was you, wasn't it?"

He knew. He had read the article and figured it out.

"I—I noticed," he said. "The way you've been around him. The way you look at me when Brett's nearby . . ."

Casey hung her head. "He took me to the beach, Chip. He kissed me. I felt awful about it . . . about doing it behind your back. I feel even worse now . . ."

"Because he's a jackass," Chip said. "Because he used you."

"Yeah." Casey could barely get the word out. She didn't dare look at him. She didn't feel she had the right to. But she had to tell him the truth. "And because you're the one who matters to me."

"I would never do that to you," he said softly, taking her hand in his. "Ever."

Casey felt her eyes water. And Chip was drawing her close, folding her in his arms.

She didn't cry. She didn't need to. She just stood there with him, feeling safe for the first time all day, rocking back and forth.

The distant din was fading a bit, and she heard a voice— someone asking for her. A familiar, confident baritone voice she sure hadn't been expecting here.

She turned suddenly.

"Casey?" said Chip.

Harrison raced by, taking her arm. "Come on, before Brianna kills him."

Casey stumbled after Harrison, calling an apology to Chip over her shoulder. Brianna was darting through the crowd in front of them, toward the sound of the voice.

Brett's.

32

"*HOW COULD YOU HAVE DONE IT, YOU CREEP?*"
Brianna screamed.

She had seen him before any of the others. She had
broken away from the well-wishers and confronted him in
front of his friends—and she didn't care who heard her.

Brett backed away from the crowd, into the cafeteria,
newly vacated. "Look, I know you're angry—"

"Angry?" Brianna echoed. "Angry doesn't begin to
cover it. How could you do that to Casey, who actually
thought you were a decent person?" She pulled a folded-
up copy of the article from her pocket and thrust it toward
him. "I keep a copy of this with me all the time. And I will
continue to all year. When I'm feeling lazy, when I start
trusting strangers again, I will use this to remind me what
kind of slime buckets there are on this earth."

"I can explain!" Brett protested. "It wasn't me."

Brianna held the article out and read: "'By Brett Masters.' Unless it was the other Brett Masters."

"I hate you," said Reese, who had rushed up with Casey and Harrison. "You knew I was kidding. You knew everything I told you at the mall was a joke. Don't even try to pretend you thought that stuff was true."

Harrison's fists were balled as he stepped toward him, with Casey only inches behind. "You goddamn motherf— "

"Listen!" Brett shouted. "I get it, okay? I get that you're all mad. I'm mad, too. *I didn't write that.* Yeah, that's my byline, and . . . a lot of the words are mine. But something happened between the time I submitted the article and the time it was printed. The article that I wrote was fun. It was tongue-in-cheek. Okay, look, I told a secret or two, but just harmless ones, to give the story some juice— otherwise Artie would never have published it. But the things about Jones Beach? Not me. The nasty stuff? Not me. Listen to me—*I'm as shocked as you are.*"

"Someone rewrote it?" Reese asked.

"Bingo," Brett replied.

"Who?" asked Harrison.

Brett shrugged. "I don't know for sure. Probably Artie. He wanted a harder article."

"He wanted sleaze," Reese said.

"He's desperate to get into journalism school. I guess he thinks this is 'investigative journalism,' but he's just— He was pushing to get me to write about the 'juicy' stuff the whole time, but I *never* thought he'd pull this." Brett shook his head sadly. "I-I had kept him posted on the research and turned in my notes when I turned in the article."

"Willing and able . . ." Casey said.

Brett's face seemed to lose color. "Like I said . . . I didn't write it . . ."

Brianna looked at Casey. She was staring Brett straight in the eye. "If you didn't write about what happened at the beach," Casey said, "how did Artie know about it?"

Brett stared at the floor. "I, um, told Artie. I told him the things you said at the mall, Reese. I told him stuff that ended up in the article. But I never thought he'd *use* it."

It killed Brianna to see the expression on Casey's face. He had taken her. Whether or not he had actually written the piece didn't really matter. He had blabbed about it to Artie.

Bragged to him. About all the info he'd been able to get from the stage manager.

"What are we going to do now?" Brianna asked.

"*Drama Clu-u-u-ub!*" Charles screamed, rushing up behind them. "Stay away from the riffraff, please. This is a glorious day! Turn around and share the lo-o-o-ove!"

Brianna took a deep breath. She looked at Casey, who held her arm out to Harrison, who held on to Reese, who linked her arms with Charles's.

Together they marched back toward the cafeteria, leaving Brett behind.

33

Theater Blog | National

Bway | Off-Broadway | Off-Off | Regional | Stock | International | News | Auditions | Agents | Scripts | AEA

Info

A Little Too Much Drama?

You remember the piece in the New York Times. The mega-musical, lavish costumes and sets, huge cast. Broadway? No, high school. The pride of Ridgeport, NY, that is, where the Drama Club's popularity rivals that of the football team in any red-blooded Division I high school in Heartland, USA.

Well, it looks like that Drama Club went one step too far this weekend, mounting an original play whose script included generous dollops of obscenity, tips on the best way to inject heroin, a graphic rape scene, and nudity. Not once, but twice.

According to an article by student Brett Masters in the Ridgeport Rambler, the school's newspaper, the club, once a bastion of rectitude and high achievement, has degenerated in recent years into a kind of private sex-and-drugs club concerned more with lighting up than lighting the lights, more with getting high than hitting the heights.

Click here for more on the new musical, "Atlantic Overtures," at the Korn Miller Playhouse in Krokory, PA!

Long Island Journal-Chronicle
School News Beat

After a flood of telephone complaints regarding a "foul," "obscenity-laced," "disgraceful" production of the Ridgeport High School Drama Club, the Ridgeport Board of Education has agreed to add a discussion of possible actions to the agenda of their meeting on Wednesday, June 4, at the Ridgeport Town Hall.

Open to the public. Refreshments will be served.

AMERICA TODAY
Letters to the Editor
May 31

Dear Editor:

I am writing to protest the actions of a few disturbed individuals who would presume to accept the "job" of moral "caretaking" of our children, subverting education in the name of cheap thrills.

If I had my way, George Levin, the teacher at Ridgeport High School, in a suburb of New York City, would not be fired. He would be arrested, tried in the highest Court, and examined for past infidelities of his "acting" career for potential reasons he might want proximity to our children. Far too many purveyors, purchasers, and practitioners of pornography and prurience have been allowed to slip through the cracks of a corrupt "educational" system decayed over decades of moral neglect. Let this be a lesson to School Districts across these United States.

We won't take it any more!!

Sincerely,
Rev. Josiah Parsifal
Bourne Falls, South Dakota

From: <scopascetic@rport.li.com>
To: CAST
Sent: Sunday, June 1, 11:35 A.M.
Subject: Fw: Fw: Fw: Re: Pettition for our children
You are not going to believe this, kids. From Mom:

----- Original Message -----
From: "Mom" <Jillian.Scopetta@arialcare.org>
To: "Charles" <scopascetic@rport.li.com>
Sent: Sunday, June 1, 9:17 A.M.
Subject: Fw: Fw: Re: Pettition for our children

> Hi, sweetie. My jaw is still hanging open over this
> one . . .
>
----- Original Message -----
From: <mombaker42367@interportal.com>

To: <Jillian.Scopetta@arialcare.org>

Sent: Sunday, June 1, 7:35 A.M.

Subject: Fw: Re: Pettition for our children

>>>

>>>> Concerned parent:

>>>> The news today is full of images both shocking

>>>> and demorallising, but none

>>>> so sad a commentery on the state of afairs

>>>> on our nations' youth then the

>>>> discovery of adult-themed sex shows on the

>>>> high school stage!! It's a manner

>>>> of UTMOST URGENCY that you sign the

>>>> bottom of this pettition and PASS

>>>> IT ONTO AT LEAST TEN OTHER'S!!! If you

>>>> are the 50th, 100th, 150th,

>>>> 200th, person, ect., forward this to

>>>> concernedparentsusa@ameritron.net.

>>>>

>>>> 1. Fielding Morrow, Bendixon, KS

>>>> 2. Wyatt Fenster, Thornbush, NV

>>>> 3. Jane Kopol Fenster, Thornbush, NV

>>>> 4. Wyatt Fenster, Jr., Thornbush, NV

. . .

Coming to school this morning had been a shock. The reporters had scared her. Kids were gathering around the mike, saying stupid things, waving at the camera and mugging like a bunch of chimpanzees.

"The dude—this supposed reverend—is from *South Dakota*?" Harrison said, reading the letter to the editor. "Where does this guy get off passing judgment on us from South Dakota?"

"And . . . *George* Levin?" Reese added. "*George?* They don't even bother getting his name right."

"Morons," Brianna grumbled.

Casey shook her head. "What I don't get is . . . these people don't even know us."

"'*Our* children . . .'" Charles said. "Like we belong to them."

"I agree this is disturbing," said Dashiell, closing his laptop. "But we can't take it personally. This has happened to us before. Press attention changes everything. You become a stereotype—whatever the media wants you to be. First we were the high school hothouse of stars. And now . . ." He shrugged.

"The porn kings," Charles remarked. "I think I liked the other description better."

"Jaaaaasper, lookee what it says here," Harrison said in his craggy-old-man voice. "Cusswords on the stage! Goldarn, must be them terrorists!"

The joke fell flat, but Casey appreciated the attempt. She looked at Chip, who sat quietly next to her. Most of all, she was worried about him. "Your awesome script . . ." she said. "They don't even mention that."

Chip shrugged. "Sticks and stones."

The door opened and Mr. Levin walked in, his eyes narrowing as he took in the sight of them hovering around Dashiell's laptop. "You've all seen the media response, I take it?"

"I knew some people in Ridgeport would be upset," Harrison said. "But *South Dakota?*"

"It's the age of the Internet," Dashiell said glumly. "Nothing is local anymore."

"Precisely," Mr. Levin agreed. "The DC has officially gone global, and I don't think this hysteria is going to die down anytime soon . . ."

Harrison winced. "I'm sorry about the F-word. It just came out."

Mr. Levin ran a hand through his hair. "I know but . . . it's not just that. We definitely crossed a few lines, and using the F-word didn't help. But even without it, I think we'd be getting a similar reaction. There are an awful lot of people who think that no one under the age of twenty-one should be exposed to material like this."

"People who want to live in a nice, fuzzy cloud," Charles muttered.

Chip spoke up, so quietly that Casey barely heard him. "Are you sorry that you let us do the play?"

"No," Mr. Levin said at once. "Not at all." He sighed deeply, then managed a smile. "No matter what happens next, I have no regrets about doing this play."

"Woo-hoo," Reese shouted uncertainly.

"You know," Harrison said, "this isn't the first time the DC has been controversial. According to Mr. Ippolito, during the production of *Hair*, in 1972, there were riots."

"I remember those stories," Reese said. "They called in the police."

"The National Guard," Charles corrected her.

"The FBI," Brianna said.

"Everyone I talked to—even the ones skittish about the raw scenes and the language—*everyone* admired the play," Mr. Levin went on. "They were won over by the script and the acting. They were moved. At least three people told me they cried." He gestured toward Dashiell's laptop. "The play they're writing about online—I don't recognize it. And I don't know who saw it."

"Are we going to be punished?" Reese said.

"Our valiant principal, Ms. Hecksher, told me quite firmly that she supports what we did," Mr. Levin replied. "She saw the play on Saturday night and said she was proud of you. And so am I. Harrison, for the idea. Casey, for having the vision to find the right playwright. Charles, for the quickest learning curve of any director I've known. The rest of you for your acting skills and tech prowess. And Chip, whose talent gave an entire community a reason to be proud."

With a flurry of keystrokes, Dashiell played a clip of "For He's a Jolly Good Fellow" on his laptop.

Reese hugged him from behind. "Corny. But we love you."

"How's this?" A few more keystrokes, and the laptop was booming a Jeff Buckley tune, "Hallelujah," Dashiell's favorite. Joyous, haunting, sad, sweet.

"That's more like it," Chip said. He began swaying to the music, singing along softly. Casey reached for his hand and closed her eyes. She felt Reese grabbing her hand, too.

It did feel good, Casey realized. Dancing for no reason felt good. The year was over. Sooner or later, the reporters would go away, the "story" would die, and all that would be left would be the truth:

1. The play had drawn a huge crowd—by word of mouth.
2. Casey had been a star.
3. Chip had shown everyone what he could do—and he looked like he had grown another inch.
4. They had put on a play that spoke the truth. And even if it was raw, it was also beautiful.

She took a deep breath and tried to let it all in.

The sharp trill of a cell phone broke the spell.

It was Mr. Levin's. Flipping it open, he said, "Levin here. Ms. Hecksher, hello. We were just . . . what's that . . . ?" His smile slowly waned. "I see . . . but how . . . Yes, of course. I'll be there."

As he folded up the phone, his face seemed to drain of color. Casey felt her own heart begin to hammer. Something was definitely wrong.

"Is everything okay?" Harrison asked.

"The board of ed," Mr. Levin said in a soft, disbelieving voice, "has been flooded with phone calls protesting the play and calling for my resignation. They're having a hearing on Wednesday."

35

CASEY GLANCED AROUND THE TOWN HALL ballroom where the board-of-ed meeting was being held and felt her stomach twist itself into a tight, hard knot. The room was enormous. And it was packed. There had to be five hundred people there.

"Move," Harrison said in a low whisper. "Spread out. Find seats. Now."

"Does everybody know what to do?" Charles asked.

"Check," Brianna said, disappearing down the center aisle.

"Yup," said Reese.

"Got it," Casey echoed. She saw a spare seat in the middle of the room and sidled her way past pairs of knees to get there.

The meeting began and then seemed to stretch on for hours. It was the most boring thing Casey had ever sat through. She tried to pay attention, but the words kept fading to nonsense. The formal intro and reading of the agenda. The town budget. School-bus routes. Whether motocross bikes made too much noise. The bond issue. Almost no one else seemed to be interested in these topics. They were all here for one thing: to be part of the judgment on Mr. Levin.

Casey couldn't get over how many people there were. Originally the meeting was to have taken place in the auditorium, but it had had to be moved to the ballroom to accommodate the crowd. She didn't even recognize most of the people there.

TV cameras lined the back of the room, and wires snaked all over, taped thickly to the floor. Reporters circulated, taking photos and footage.

She looked over toward Chip, who was sitting across the room to her left, bright-eyed and attentive, taking notes on the details of the bond issue.

Figured.

Charles was behind her somewhere. Harrison was to her right, barely visible behind a woman with big hair. Reese and Dashiell and Brianna were there, too, but she couldn't see them.

"And now," intoned the board president, a balding guy with half-glasses and jowls that shook when he looked up, "our last item on the agenda, the matter of Mr. Gregory Levine, teacher at the, uh, high school. Is Mr. Levine here? Ah yes, welcome, sir, and we, uh, thank you for all the pleasure you've given the community over the years, et cetera."

Click. Click click click click.

The room exploded with a flurry of flash photos.

"Thank you, Mr. Fahnestock," said Mr. Levin, who was sitting up front, his hands folded in his lap. "Respectfully . . . it's *Levin*."

He looked tense and formal, his hair newly cut, his suit and tie perfect. Like a prisoner before sentencing, Casey thought.

"Yes, excuse me, Mr. Levin," Mr. Fahnestock said, leaning forward. "Now, we, uh, have the greatest respect for you, sir, but there have been some serious charges regarding a possible, uh, shall we say, breach of trust with the community vis-à-vis the participation of the students in a dramatic production that, uh, violates standards of community decency and so forth. Before I give you a chance to respond to this, I would like to open the floor to any member of the public who has seen the show and would, uh, like to comment. I'll have hands only, please."

"Animal acts belong in the barnyard!" someone cried out from the back.

"OH!" That was Charles, trying to choke back a laugh.

"We want excellence, not X-ratings!" came another shout.

Whack! Whack! Mr. Fahnestock smacked an old gavel on his table. "Hands only, please! Yes, you, sir, with the orange shirt . . ."

Up shot a man with a shock of white hair and a string tie fastened by a metal clasp around his neck. "I think we can all agree that a high school is a place where education is foremost, in a wholesome environment free from filth and negative influences from subversive elements in society—"

"Sir, did you see the production in question?" Mr. Fahnestock asked.

"—and any so-called teacher who would allow lewd acts between minors to occur in public for all to see—"

"Sir, *did you see the play?*"

"A person doesn't need to see filth to smell it—"

"Yes, you do, for the purposes of this hearing," Mr. Fahnestock said. "Er, see the play, that is. With all due respect, sir, please sit. You in the yellow blouse . . ."

Casey smiled. This Fahnestock guy wasn't so bad after all.

"I saw the play," said a youngish woman with a little kid squirming in her arms. "It was raw. There were a few words that made me wince. It sure wasn't like anything we did in *my* high school. But I wish we had. We would have learned so much from doing something real—something written by a kid, about things kids care about."

There was a smattering of applause, and a few jeers, and Mr. Fahnestock continued calling on people, one after the other:

"There are plenty of published plays, award-winning plays, tested by time. Why couldn't they use one of those . . . ?"

"Shakespeare! Andrew Lloyd Webber! *That's* theater . . . !"

"It was okay. I don't see what the fuss was all about. Kids use these words every day and see people use them on TV . . ."

"Where is God in all of this . . . ?"

"When they're over eighteen, in college, they can do what they want. But not here . . ."

Poor Mr. Levin sat through it all, his shoulders slumping. Occasionally he would turn and muster a brave smile for Casey and the others.

She looked at the clock. The discussion of the play had been going for ten minutes.

Her heart raced. Ten minutes was the signal.

"Um, hello? Can I say something?" Harrison's voice rang out.

Begin.

Casey tensed. Harrison was the perfect one to start. He was in his speak-to-the-last-row mode. "I think this is all about right and wrong," he said. "Sometimes it's easy. Like, when a little kid runs into the street and the mom is screaming—you know what to do. Even though it's not your kid, you grab him. That's the *right* thing to do."

Click click click.

The photographers spun around as Brianna began:

"But when the problem is something you don't understand," she called out, "something you don't see— what do you say? What's the right thing to do? Do you keep it inside? Do you say something?"

"Of course!" shouted the man with the orange shirt. "You say something!"

Now Barry was talking, from clear over on the left side

of the room. "Society tells you not to open your mouth. They'll say some things are not appropriate. Those things will make others uncomfortable. So you keep your words inside. But you know what? That's wrong. 'Cause silence is about fear. And fear kills you inside."

"Which is why we're here!" said another one of the complainers from behind Casey. "To exercise our free speech!"

"So the important thing is to speak," Jenny piped up. "To speak to *someone*. It's all about expression, you know? It's about speaking the truth—or what you *believe* is the truth—"

Now.

"Because by speaking you keep your mind open and your soul alive," Casey said. "And sometimes you discover that maybe you're wrong. Maybe everything you're thinking is totally whack. And maybe not. But you got to *let it out!*"

Click click click.

"Amen!" shouted another voice.

A burst of applause broke out. Casey could see Harrison moving through the seats, heading for the aisle.

Another board member, a cramped-looking guy with thick glasses, stood up and announced, "I think the press can see tonight that not *all* of our kids are like the ones portrayed in the media, that some of them embody the values we cherish in this community . . ."

Casey got up and excused herself, squeezing past the knees of the people in her row. Brianna was moving, too, and Charles and Casey. Reese had on an outfit so conservative—a straight gray skirt and pale lavender sweater set—that Casey almost didn't recognize her. Chip was there, too, and Barry and Jenny.

"Sir?" Harrison called out. "We *are* those kids in the media."

The crowd began murmuring, bewildered. The TV cameras snapped around to catch Harrison. A photographer raced down the aisle.

Mr. Fahnestock banged his gavel loudly. "Quiet, please!"

Casey joined the rest of them in front of the audience, just below the stage where the board was seated. "The words we just said were taken from the play *Early Action*," Harrison announced, "and written by Chip Duggan, who is standing next to me."

"They were spoken on Thursday and Saturday night at the Ridgeport High School cafeteria," Charles explained. "*That* was what the audience was hearing—a monologue from the script, word for word, spoken by the main character but divided up tonight among all of us."

"If you believe what we just said," Brianna spoke up, "then you believe in free speech."

"And if you believe in free speech for you, then you believe in it for all," Harrison said. "Including your children—us."

"Our play wasn't about shock, or thumbing noses at anyone," Chip said. "It's about what we're doing now—about the importance of expression. And what happens when you block it. About the death of the soul. How one young man brings himself back from despair. How he deals with a tragedy that nearly ruins his life."

"It's serious stuff, yo!" a voice blurted from the back of the room.

Kyle. Casey smiled. She didn't realize he was here, too.

"And it's *this* man," Reese said, gesturing to Mr. Levin, "who saw the potential of the play and let us put it on."

That was the cue to leave, and as they did the DC members shook Mr. Levin's hand as they passed. "Thanks," he mouthed to each of them.

Heads turned as they proceeded together to the back of the big hall, where they stood among the standing-room-only crowd.

"If these are the children who did this," a voice shouted, "why is there such a fuss?"

"Is best play anywhere!" bellowed Mr. Michaels. "Is better than TV! *Is make me cry!*"

Now people were shouting all at once:

"They could have done the same thing without profanity!"

"I found it offensive!"

"I saw it! And it was fantastic!"

"You can't believe in free speech and try to censor this play!"

"QUIET!" Mr. Fahnestock shouted. "Everyone be seated!"

A man whom Casey recognized as one of the members of the town council raised his hand, and Mr. Fahnestock said, "All right, I'll take one last comment. Councilman?"

"The question is not whether or not *Early Action* is a good play," the councilman began in a reasonable tone. "And I don't think the issue is free speech. The question here is about what is appropriate for a high school, and about the judgment of a member of the faculty. My son brought home a copy of the *Ridgeport Rambler*, and I read Brett Masters's article. I can tell you, I was very distressed to learn about what really goes on in the Drama Club. Mr. Levin is obviously not guiding or supervising his charges properly, and that's why we wound up with a play that, despite its merits, is simply not appropriate for a high school."

Casey felt the shift in the room, and glanced at the others. Dashiell was shaking. Brianna looked like she was going to scream. Harrison looked like he was going to explode. Chip just looked doomed.

They'd had a chance, Casey thought, before the councilman mentioned Brett's article. Now it felt like they had no chance at all. Mr. Levin would be fired, and it would all be because *she* had a stupid crush and suggested that Brett write about the DC.

"Thank you," said Mr. Fahnestock. "I think we have heard enough. I move that the board take a vote on the matter of the employment of Mr. Greg Levine—"

"Levin," said Mr. Levin.

"Uh, yes, my apologies." Mr. Fahnestock turned to the other board members and they began to murmur among themselves.

Casey bit her nails. She could see her mom smiling. Tossing her a thumbs-up. Brianna's parents were there, too. And Harrison's. Chip rested his arm on Casey's shoulder. Brianna's fingers were crossed. Harrison closed his eyes.

It must have been five minutes, but it seemed like an hour before Mr. Fahnestock finally stepped to the front of the room again.

The place fell silent. Mr. Fahnestock cleaned his glasses and surveyed the crowd uncomfortably. "We have a count—uh, in favor of retaining the services of Mr. Levin, three. In favor of terminating said services . . . three."

"*Whaaat?*" Charles blurted.

"It's a tie," Mr. Fahnestock said.

"What does that mean?" Reese asked.

An argument erupted between two couples on the left side. People were laughing derisively, shouting reactions, talking aloud to one another.

WHACK! WHACK! "Quiet!" Mr. Fahnestock shouted. "This is, uh, unprecedented, and we will have to adjourn for further—"

"EXCUSE ME! *EXCUSE ME!*" From behind Casey came a loud, frantic cry. The crowd began to part, looking toward the entrance.

Barging through, red-faced and sweaty, was Brett. "Did they take the vote yet?"

"It was a tie," Harrison said.

"Crap," Brett replied.

"What are you doing here?" Brianna said with disdain.

"Trying to make up for what Artie—and I—did to you," Brett replied, then broke away to run down the aisle. "UH, BOARD? MR. FAHNESTOCK?" As everyone turned around to look, Brett called over his shoulder, "Come on, Mom!"

Brett's mother looked as though she had just stepped out of a meeting. She was dressed in a gray pin-striped suit and designer heels. Her hair, a little unkempt, was held in place by a barrette, and she marched down the aisle, looking a little flustered. "Sorry," she said. "My plane was delayed. I wouldn't have gotten here at all if my son hadn't been waiting with the car—am I too late?"

"We, uh, just cast a vote," Mr. Fahnestock said, "on the question of—"

"The firing of Mr. Levin?" Mrs. Masters replied. "Well, I have been following that one closely. I read my son's article about it—and frankly, sir, I find the whole thing disgusting!"

Casey blanched.

"Oh God, no . . ." Charles murmured.

"Didn't he explain it to her?" Harrison whispered.

"Nuked again," Reese said.

Mrs. Masters walked to the front of the room and turned to the crowd. "May I ask a question? How many of you in the audience are in favor of firing Mr. Levin?"

Hands shot into the air, hundreds of them, far more than half.

"Of those people, how many actually live in Ridgeport?"

A murmur went through the crowd. Hands raised again, slower this time.

And not more than half of the previous number.

"And of those," Mrs. Masters said, "how many saw the play in question?"

Seven.

Casey counted them twice. Seven hands!

Mrs. Masters nodded. "Full disclosure—I saw the play, on opening night, before my business trip. And I must tell you, I have been thinking about it ever since." She walked over to Mr. Levin and looked him in the eye. "And if we as a community can vote to destroy a resource like this man, who allows education—real education—to flourish, then wherever he goes, my family will move."

"Er, I take it that's a vote to retain?" Mr. Fahnestock asked.

"It is," Mrs. Masters said. "We've been fortunate to have a teacher as fine as Mr. Levin running the Drama Club. I only hope we'll be fortunate enough to keep him."

"Four to three—Mr. Levin stays!" Mr. Fahnestock shouted.

"YEEEEAAAHHHHH!"

Casey was running, running and dodging, pushing her way through strangers and friends until she got to the front of the room.

She was the first one to put her arms around Mr. Levin. And she held on tight.

weasels ripped my quivering flesh

june 5
ok, what is THE biggest pain-in-the-butt question i've been asked ALL DAY? "WHY DID YOU WRITE IT?"

and the answer is, "I DIDN'T." Yes, the rambler article has my name on it. but no, owing to circumstances out of my control, an article with a HEAVY agenda was published falsely under my name. ok, here's the other question: "HOW MUCH OF IT IS TRUE?"

answer: none of the skanky stuff. NONE. i have been living, breathing, working with these dudes day & night. they kick ass & the play was AMAZING.

MY question: How many of those complaining people actually SAW the play? NONE! read closely. & what did you hear on TV? a lot of "i didn't actually SEE the play, but ..."

talk to someone who really saw it. who isn't stupid and brainwashed. who understands that high-school kids don't belong in playpens.

my favorite blog sites:

kickassjonay (my bro)

ridgemidge

dcrules

scopascetic charlettes

ms. ahmed's eighth period creative writing class

dylanthomas lives!

nycpoetry forums

nuyoricancafe

theaterslut

that scottish play

allsondheim allthetime

"Brett quit the newspaper?" Harrison asked.

"That's what I heard," Reese said. "There was a huge argument. He really gave it to Artie, and told him he was going to write an exposé about the *Rambler*. Then Artie offered to print it. He loved the idea. He thought it would totally nail his application to journalism school."

"They deserve each other," said Brianna.

"We have to give him some credit," Harrison said. "He's trying to help us. And his mom is the bomb."

"He still has a long way to go," Brianna shot back.

Sitting at the end of the table at Kostas Korner, Casey felt Chip squeezing her hand. She squeezed back.

Mr. Michaels and Niko the waiter appeared from around the corner with trays full of steaming food. "Here you are!" Mr. Michaels boomed. "Cheeseburger, moussaka, pastitsio, turkey club, macaronia, bacon burger . . . on the house! Nobody pay! Today is big day for Haralambos and the Drama Club!"

"Really?" Casey asked.

"That is sooooo cute," said Reese.

"A shout-out for Mr. Michaels!" Charles said, leaping up from his chair. "WOO-HOOOO!"

Mr. Michaels threw his head back and laughed. "God bless America and don't forget Director Tsarles!" With that, he gave Charles a big bear hug.

"He likes me," Charles said, sinking back into his seat.

"He always did," said Harrison.

Chip rose from his seat, banging on a glass for silence and then lifting a mug of Coke. "Guys, I just want to give a toast to the two most important people here. First of all,

Mr. Levin, for letting us go through with this in the first place—even putting his job on the line!"

A scream went up from the table, and Mr. Levin grinned.

"But the play wouldn't have happened without one person in this room," Chip continued, "who convinced me I was good enough. Who made me realize that criticism makes you stronger—and that real expression starts when you face the truth. And who is not only the most talented actor, but the nicest person I know. A toast to Casey Chang!"

"WOOOOOOOO!"

The cheer was so loud that Niko the waiter dropped a tray of Greek salad, sending cubes of feta cheese sliding across the floor.

"NIKO, YOU FIRED!" Mr. Michaels shouted, and then grabbed the waiter by the shoulder and laughed and laughed.

By instinct, Harrison and Niko both knelt to pick up the dropped food. And Mr. Michaels joined them. Along with Charles.

Chip turned to Casey and smiled. She hugged him and he planted a big kiss on her lips, to another cheer, this one extending into the restaurant itself.

Casey blushed. It felt good. She decided that feeling good, tonight, was the first order of business.

Everything else could wait.

Epilogue

EARLY ACTION WAS A FIRST FOR RIDGEPORT.
They put a special plaque with a photo in the case, just
for Chip.

People are still talking about it. And I imagine they will
for a long time.

I have to say, it wasn't a totally happy ending, though.

For one thing, my dad really was pissed about the
spilled Greek salad. I think he actually deducted the cost
of it from Niko's pay. The Drama Club was going to take
up a collection and pay him back, but instead we decided
to give him a humongous tip the next time we eat in the
diner.

Mr. Levin survived this incident. Just as Mrs. Masters
had shown, at least half of the complaints were from out-

of-towners. And most of the rest were from Ridgeport old-timers who hadn't seen the show. The local news carried a follow-up, playing clips of our "presentation" at the board meeting. I could have delivered my lines slower and with better emphasis, but that's another story.

Ms. Hecksher welcomed Mr. Levin back to school over the loudspeaker and made a big fuss over what a hero he was. That was sweet.

As for our new resident genius, Chip, he had to pull all the Post-it notes out of his *Fiske Guide to Colleges*. He's no longer looking at schools for political science or engineering, or whatever he was into. His eyes are on the theater departments now, and he's taken to wearing T-shirts from Carnegie Mellon and Juilliard and NYU, which in his research he has found to be "conducive to playwrighting."

His eyes are also on Casey, a lot. She seems pleased about this, but with her, it's hard to tell.

Brianna thinks Casey's still in love with Brett, but I don't agree. Brett really burned her. Burned all of us, really. Yes, I believe his story. I believe Artie took his article and twisted it. Brett even showed us the draft he turned in to the *Rambler*—and, just as he said, it was fun, totally tongue-in-cheek, with none of the really skanky details. But Brett's interest in Casey disappeared after the show. I think he was using her to get info about the DC, plain and simple. And I can't respect that. Besides, he did tell Artie about Brett and Casey at Jones Beach—and that was not kosher, period.

For all I know, Brianna is the one who's hot over Brett.

She talks about him enough. For someone I've known so long, I still don't understand her. She's still mad that we haven't really "talked it out." About what happened between us. I tell her that she wasn't around much during rehearsals, and when she finally was, she was too busy.

She doesn't buy it. But that's the way it goes with her.

Brett has not stopped in his campaign to get revenge on Artie Sprengle. The dude is a little OCD about it. I wish he'd give it up. Artie's walking around like a whipped puppy these days.

I still think back to the day this all started. Doing an unofficial, independent play seemed like such a no-brainer. But now I lie awake thinking about what a fool I was. How unbelievably naive. I've asked myself a million times, would I have done it if I knew what the risks were— trying to pull together an unknown play from a first-time high school playwright with a first-time director . . . dragging the Drama Club through the mud in national media . . . putting Mr. Levin's career at risk?

Yeah. I would.

In a New York minute.